Praise for "Sticky Wicket, Vol. 1,Watkins At Bat."

"Sticky Wicket, Vol. 1, Watkins At Bat, is a wonderful addition to contemporary cricket literature. The plot weaves the age-old themes of the sport into modern life.... This first volume is a strong opener for what should be a successful series."

-Paul Hensley, president of C.C. Morris Cricket Library
Haverford College, Haverford, PA.

*

"The scheming plots involved in getting some of the players, both young and old, away from their wives to the playing field... will surely give any reader who enjoys a good laugh lots to laugh about."

-Carol Quash, Trinidad Guardian

*

"To the cricket-initiated, the volume is distilled mirth."

-Tom Baldwin, Gannett News Service, and author of "Big Storm, Small Ship."

*

"A bit of Watkins resides in all our hearts and homes. An entertaining narrative about the interaction of cricketing families in the United States, chronicled in a jocular way that makes reading *Sticky Wicket* fun and a must read for all cricket enthusiasts."

-Shelton Glasgow, president, Garden State Cricket League; regional director, Atlantic region of the United States of America Cricket Association, & USACA board member.

*

"*Watkins At Bat,* the first in the *Sticky Wicket* trilogy, is an entertaining romp with a motley cast of characters by an author whose love of the game of cricket is evident on every page. A wonderful adventure!"

- Glenn Walker, owner/moderator of Writer Circle:
http://groups.yahoo.com/group/writercircle/

*

"The author has used his favorite game as a metaphor to bring his feisty characters to life in a sparkling and humorous manner that is a delight. Ride along with Rouse's imagination in *Sticky Wicket, Vol. 1, Watkins At Bat,* and hurry; the 'cricket train' is about to leave the station. Be on it!"

-Paul Gordon, author of the novels "Concrete Solution" "Van Gogh's Last Painting" and "Bogey-man on Gaston Street."

*

"It was hilarious reading how these fellows got away from their wives on Sundays to enjoy a game that we all grew up playing. I also was moved to see how cricket brought so many different races together."

-Adrian Rahim, captain Jersey City Cricket Club, Jersey City, New Jersey.

*

"I read the novel during a flight from Philadelphia to Jamaica and laughed so hard, and so often, that passengers near me must have thought I had lost it."

-Paul Francis, co-founder Echelon Cricket Club, Voorhees, New Jersey.

*

"I thought I was reliving my playing experiences in America while reading of the exploits of Frederick A. Watkins. It was hard to put down once I started it. I finished the book in one sitting. I was glad I didn't have to go out to bat during that time!"

-Dan Ruparel, president, The Littleton Cricket Club & Colorado Junior Cricket Association, and former president, Colorado Cricket League.

*

"I enjoyed reading this first volume quite a bit and look forward to reading further volumes."

-Ron Knight, umpire, Mid-Atlantic Cricket Conference, Chapel Hill, North Carolina.

EWART ROUSE

STICKY WICKET
Vol. 1

watkins at bat

Cover Design by: Sanya Dockery
Book Design, Layout & Typesetting by: Sanya Dockery

Published by: LMH Publishing Limited
7 Norman Road,
LOJ Industrial Complex
Building 10
Kingston C.S.O., Jamaica
Tel: 876-938-0005; 938-0712
Fax: 876-759-8752
Email: lmhbookpublishing@cwjamaica.com
Website: www.lmhpublishing.com

Printed in U.S.A.   ISBN: 978-976-8202-40-6

This book is dedicated to my father,
Alexander Abraham Rouse,
cricket enthusiast who taught me the love of the game,
on his 100th birthday.

ACKNOWLEDGMENTS

The author wishes to thank the following people for their invaluable contributions: Ben Acosta, Fran Metzman, Maryliz Clark, Margo M. Foster, Porus Cooper, Carol Smith, Amber Samaroo, Danny Patel, and Maura Ciccarell-Green and her husband John Green.

Foreword

When immigrants from the West Indies, India, Pakistan and England settle in Fernwood, South Jersey, USA, they want to play the game of their youth: cricket. The obstacles they face are the theme of the Sticky Wicket trilogy, *Watkins At Bat, Watkins Fights Back* and *Watkins' Final Inning*.

Not only must Frederick A. Watkins, the protagonist who is of West Indian heritage, fight with his African-American wife, Gina, to spend his weekends on the cricket field, he and his ragtag team from many lands must vie with local officials of the suburban town who prefer that only Little League baseball teams play on their field.

In addition to facing the challenges of prejudice and political opportunists, the Fernwood Cricket Club must also wrestle with the problem of aging players, personal foibles and distractions, and pull of family who want their time and affection.

How Watkins juggles a cast of multi-ethnic, multi-national characters from all walks of life to keep the cricket club alive, and his marriage intact, leads the reader through a true "sticky wicket."

watkins at bat

9:00 a.m., Sunday, April 29

W hen the telephone rang and Gina answered, Frederick A. Watkins could have sworn from the way his wife flinched that it was an obscene caller. It was much worse:

"Someone with a Jamaican accent says he wants to speak to Freddie Watkins." Gina bristled as she slid – rather than handed – the cordless phone across the breakfast table, suddenly not a friendly bone in her body. "It had better not be about another cricket match."

Watkins sought with a nervous smile to assure his wife that her angst was without merit. It would have been common knowledge in the New Jersey cricket community by now that he had retired from the sport. The emotional farewell party for him on the team's home field at the end of last season had been written up in the league's newsletter. It was quite a splash – a color photo of him propped up on his beloved, oversized bat at the wicket, broad-brimmed hat tilted at a rakish angle, arms folded over blue-and-red blazer, legs crossed. The caption read:

The legendary Frederick A. Watkins, manager of Fernwood Cricket Club, hangs it up after twenty-five years of dedicated service to cricket in America. Thanks for the memories, old chap, and happy retirement.

"Hello," Watkins said.

The caller identified himself as Victor Stuart, captain of the Jamaica Rebels Cricket Club in Newark. "Nice day for cricket," Stuart added.

While savoring the specialty coffee and dry toast with his wife at the kitchen table, sun streaking through slanted blinds, that thought hadn't escaped Watkins. After four consecutive weekends of heavy rain and a freak snowstorm, this last weekend of April was proving to be a dandy – bright, clean skies, with just the right chill in the air, the sort of weekend for spring cleaning, cutting the grass, starting a garden, browsing at flea markets.

And, yes, playing the game of his youth.

Watkins nudged the thought aside. "Guess you haven't heard," he said. "I'm officially retired."

"Congratulations," Stuart replied, with no great enthusiasm. "Now, how about some directions to your grounds? Proper directions."

Heavy emphasis on the word *proper*.

Watkins thought it a small favor. This very well could be his last unofficial act on behalf of his club. He gave the directions.

"Thanks," Stuart said. "Now, tell your players don't forget to bring their helmets. We'll supply the bandages. We'll also provide small stretchers, so if they need extra small, they'll have to bring their own."

Watkins cleared his throat of a frog that wasn't there and forced himself to chuckle. "You're joking, right?"

"Jamaica Rebels don't joke!"

Click.

Watkins simmered.

Gina had busied herself loading the dishwasher.

"What's that all about?"

"You're right," he said. "It was about a cricket match. The captain of Jamaica Rebels asked for directions to our grounds, then threatened to knock our players' blocks off with their fastballs."

"Isn't cricket supposed to be a gentlemen's game?"

"Not with those Jamaicans."

"All this fighting over a silly game."

"Yeah, a silly game," he said, mimicking her pooh-poohing tone. Stuart's fighting words had had the intended effect of rattling him, and Gina had hit a sore spot with her put-down of the game. Time was when she enjoyed listening to his reports on the shenanigans on the sports front, but now, after twenty-five years of marriage and cricket, she had made a one-hundred-eighty-degree turn.

"Thank God you've decided to give up your manager's job this year," Gina said. "Let the other club members deal with those bullies from up north." She turned on the dishwasher. "We better get ready for church.... Fred, where are you going?"

Watkins was on his feet, pushing past her. "Got to alert the guys that Jamaica Rebels are coming to play dirty."

"Make it snappy," she called out. "We don't want to be late for church."

Her cabin fever at high pitch, Gina was raring to go again. They had spent Saturday hitting the yard sales, followed by a brisk trek through the park. Gina was into fitness and had decided he should lose the tire around his middle. She had set the pace in her new hiking gear, hair done up in a bun, arms pumping in military precision. She had rewarded him with dinner at the Olive Garden and a movie. Today she was going to follow up by dragging him out to church. The standard excuse that he needed time to finish his novel didn't cut it anymore. With retirement, she had lectured, he had all the time in the world to write.

Watkins' head throbbed as he settled into the chair behind the desk of his basement office. He dialed Vijay Patel's number.

"Hello." The female voice was tiny, wavering and foreign.

"This is Frederick Alfred Watkins."

"What do you want?" Mrs. Patel said.

"May I speak with your husband?"

"I'm his wife," Mrs. Patel said, now very assertive.

"I know." An image – nineteen, half-child, half-woman, luminous eyes staring out of a rounded face half-covered by a sari – flashed through his mind. Her name was Aisha. She was Muslim, which meant no alcohol or dancing at the wedding. Patel was Hindu and his folks vegetarians. On his return from their honeymoon, Patel made it up to the hard-drinking, meat-eating West Indian invitees by taking them out to a strip joint for dinner. "We met at the wedding."

"What do you want?"

"May I speak to your husband?"

"I'm his wife," Mrs. Patel said again.

Watkins reluctantly stated his business: Vijay Patel had agreed at the end of last season to take over from him as club manager. As part of his responsibilities, Patel was to mobilize the team and see to it that the wicket was ready for today's game. He wanted to speak to Patel about the game.

"My husband busy," said Mrs. Patel. "He can't come to game."

"May I speak with him anyway?"

"I'm his wife."

Exasperated, Watkins gave up on Mrs. Patel and telephoned Emile Pierre.

Angie picked up and she had no qualms – at least, Watkins didn't detect any in her voice – in letting him know her husband's whereabouts: Pierre was out front cutting the grass.

"I'll get him for you," she said.

It was the response Watkins expected. Pierre and Angie were from Antigua. Unlike their Asian counterparts, West Indian women knew – regardless of how they might feel about the time their spouses spent away from home at cricket - that there would be hell to pay for sabotaging any communication between them and their club mates.

"Nice day for cricket." Pierre sounded breathless.

"Got the troops ready for today's game?" Watkins asked the team skipper and unofficial attorney.

"Today! Do we have a game today?"

"Didn't you get a call from Vijay?"

"I haven't heard from Patel since he got married. Hold on."

Watkins heard Pierre ask Angie in the background whether Vijay Patel had called and she said no.

"Who are we supposed to be playing, anyway?"

Watkins told him, as well as about the threat by the Jamaica Rebels captain. "He's still pissed off about what we did to them last year," Watkins added. "Maybe I ought to call back and cancel."

"And let them think we're cowards? No way!"

"It's a 1 o'clock start." Watkins checked the wall clock. "It's now 9:15. It would be tough to put together a team, plus fix the wicket, at such short notice."

"Tell you what," Pierre said. "I'll go down to the grounds and begin working on the wicket while you call up the guys."

Watkins agreed to make the calls. It was the least he could do, his retired status notwithstanding.

"See you at the grounds," Pierre said, and hung up.

See you at the grounds? Watkins felt the rush as he booted up the computer and called up the club's membership roster.

Shane Asquith, the lone Brit in the club, topped the list.

Cindy, his American wife, answered and reported that her husband had gone jogging with their two daughters.

Watkins chatted with her a bit about her and her husband's respective careers. Cindy said that her teaching job was the usual, but that the computer consulting firm she had helped her husband establish was on the skids.

He said he was sorry to hear.

"I suppose you're calling about cricket," she said.

"Shane was wondering when you'd call. He's been oiling his bat and practicing with the girls in the yard."

Watkins was pleasantly surprised. The club had had several Englishmen over the quarter-century of its existence, but only for brief stints. One day they were playing for Fernwood, the next they had signed up with an all-British team in Philadelphia. Called itself Mad Dogs something. Maybe it was a comfort thing.

Cindy promised to give Shane his message about the game and said she and "the girls" might drop by to watch.

Watkins put Asquith down as a "definite" for the game and his wife and two teen daughters as possible cheerleaders.

Next was Fitzroy Chong, aka the Black Chinaman.

The Barbados native picked up on the first ring.

"Great! What time?" he said when told about the game.

"The usual 1 o'clock coin toss," Watkins said. "But we need you down at the grounds right away to help prepare the wicket."

A heavy silence, followed by an abrupt: "Who's this?"

"What do you mean 'Who's this?'"

"To whom am I speaking?" Chong had dropped the Barbados accent for the formal tone of an English butler.

"Cut it out!"

"I beg your pardon?" Chong was really laying it on thick.

"Okay, this is Freddie Watkins of the Fernwood Cricket Club," Watkins said.

"You want my brother, mate."

Watkins wasn't amused. "I just told you about the game and you said great. I ask you to go to the grounds to do some work and you give me this bullshit about having a brother newly arrived from London."

It was maddening, but every team has a Fitzroy Chong. He is the player who shows up to play after his teammates have prepared the wicket. If he arrives early and there is still work to be done, he hides out in the parking lot or circles the area in his car. At the end of the game, after generous helpings of the refreshments, he sneaks out before the cleanup starts.

"I play tennis." Chong wasn't about to let up. "I thought you were calling about a tennis game. My brother is the cricket player. Let me get some writing tablet." The sound of paper being shuffled. "Will you spell your name for me, old chap?"

"W-A-T-K-I-N-S."

"Blower, please?"

Watkins gave him the telephone number.

"Splendid," said Chong. "My brother will be in touch, I'm sure."

Watkins put the lazy Barbadian down as a "definite," and proceeded down the list.

"Aren't you getting ready?"

The voice at his back startled him. Watkins tried to switch screens but the computer froze. He spun to face his wife, at the same time maneuvering his body to shield the screen.

Gina had pulled her hair back and wore a red hat with a feather in the crown. She had traded the loose-fitting housecoat for a black dress that accentuated her trim figure. She towered over him on high heels.

"The guys didn't know about the game," Watkins said. "Patel never got in touch with them."

"That has nothing to do with you," Gina said. "We're already late for church. And don't forget: Maggie and Stephen are coming down with our grandson. If it gets warm enough maybe we can put something on the grill..."

She stopped, leaned her head to one side and squinted.

Her expression told Watkins she had caught a glimpse of the screen.

She wheeled him aside to get a better look and recoiled. "Fred, what's going on?"

"I'm trying to mobilize the team," he said. "Do you mind if I skip church today?"

Her dimpled cheeks quivered, and her dark eyes grew moist. "I don't understand." Fire rose in her throat. "After twenty-five years of deserting your family every weekend from spring through fall, you were going to hang it up this season. Now, the first nice weekend of spring, the phone rings, and your promise is out the window."

"Just this once... Gina, please don't look at me that way!"

"Fred, answer me this question: What's more important to you, your cricket club or your marriage?"

"What sort of question is that!"

"I need to know."

"I won't answer a question like that."

"You just did!"

Watkins sprang to his feet and rushed to block her retreat. "Gina, what's gotten into you? I haven't been to church in a while. What difference does one Sunday make?"

"You promised, Fred! No more cricket. I believed you."

"One last game," he said. "That's all I ask. One last game."

"Why even bother? You never win."

"For the record, we did win one game last year."

"By default," she said. "You gave the Jamaicans bad directions to your grounds so they'd arrive late."

"That's their side of the story. The truth is they got lost."

"They did arrive late," she said, "and you did claim the points by default. That made them mad. And they're still mad. Isn't that why Stuart just threatened to knock your blocks off? They're coming to get even. This is supposed to be some grudge match."

Watkins stared at his wife in genuine surprise. "I wish you'd stop eavesdropping on my conversations!"

"Don't have to," Gina said. "For twenty-five years, that's all you talk about on the phone. Even in your sleep. Who's mad because he got dropped from the team.

Another fight over the umpire's decision. Another move to sack the captain. Everything takes a backseat to cricket in this house. Even your daughter. You missed each turning point in Maggie's life. You weren't there the day she was born. You weren't there to see her turn her head, or roll over in her crib for the first time, or crawl, or take that first step. You almost missed escorting her up the aisle. All because of cricket. And now you are about do the same with your grandson...."

Watkins hung his head. Once Gina started down that road, he knew there was no stopping her. The litany of his other sins flowed: the missed birthdays and wedding anniversary dinners, to say nothing about Sunday church.

They had been over each transgression before. How many times, and in how many ways, did he have to say he was sorry? Sure, they had agreed at the end of last season that it was all water under the bridge and she had accepted his promise to make amends now that he was newly retired from the ad agency. Now was supposed to be their time. Still, all he was asking for was one last game. Surely, he wasn't being unreasonable.

"I just don't understand what you get out of it," Gina continued to rave, raking up those embers to start a new fire, recalling old ghosts. "You no longer get to play, yet you persist in running yourself ragged for the team. And for what, Fred? For what?" Gina drew a very deep breath, replenishing oxygen now that she was deflated and near gasping.

"Look how you've upset yourself," Watkins said, moving to stroke her shoulders. "There's no need for this."

She pulled away from him. "I'm so sick and tired of it." She clenched her fists, fighting to control herself. "You have to decide, Fred. Do you love cricket more than you love the Lord and your family?"

"I don't like ultimatums."

Gina proudly pulled herself together, raising her chin better to look down her nose at him. Then there was something in her eyes that he hadn't seen before: pity. At that moment, Gina seemed to justify her own irrational behavior by pitying him.

"Goodbye, Fred."

"Stop being so melodramatic," he said. "This is not a matter of life and..."

Gina did an about-face that would have put a drill team to shame, marched around him and out of the room, slamming the door behind her. Moments later, the house vibrated a second time when she banged the front door shut. He heard the squeal of tires, a crash, and more squeals.

Watkins looked out. The BMW was missing from alongside his wagon in the driveway. There were tire marks in the freshly cut grass and the freestanding mailbox lay on its side.

Watkins eased himself down. Gina had been behaving irrationally since she turned forty-eight. Watkins told himself he felt for her and the body changes she was experiencing. He sincerely did, but rationalized that she knew even before they were married that cricket took priority over everything but dire emergencies. Of course, he was a young man then, with an athlete's body. In those early days Gina, too, was very much part of the club and the game, keeping the books and helping organize social events for players and supporters. Back then, before the influx of immigrants and the birth of the New Jersey Cricket League, the club played friendly games against teams made up mostly of immigrants at area universities – University of Pennsylvania, Haverford, Rutgers, Princeton and the Lawrence Preparatory School in central New Jersey.

Gina used to enjoy the camaraderie with the mixed bag of players from such widely scattered, former British Commonwealth countries as India and Pakistan, England, and the West Indies islands – different races, religions, ethnic backgrounds, and walks of life. They had arrived in the United States as students, contract employees, visitors and permanent residents, settling initially in the inner cities of the Northeast and, over time, ending up here in Fernwood, a South Jersey suburb of Philadelphia.

Here in suburbia, mimicking the lifestyles of their American neighbors with their two-and-a-half kids and a dog in subdivisions with multi-car garages and manicured lawns, you might say they had achieved the so-called American Dream. They were Americans, very much part of the mainstream in every way.

Except one.

Cricket.

Like music and food, the sports of your youth stay in your blood. Cricket was the game of their youth in their native lands. And cricket was the game of their adulthood in their adopted homeland, a way of life that linked their small, diverse group.

In the beginning, the wives and girlfriends brought their native dishes to the park, along with the kids, and they made a picnic of it. Gina, the sole American among them in the early days, was part of that big, extended family. Then the novelty wore off for the women, and the fun went out entirely when the club joined the New Jersey Cricket League, and the competition and their travel schedule grew more rigorous.

Watkins tried to look at it from his wife's perspective. As an African American, Gina didn't grow up with the sport. To him, it was a way of life; to her, a form of entertainment and relaxation that she had outgrown and wanted to move away from.

Gina surely was overreacting, Watkins told himself. Her "Goodbye, Fred" was pure theater, a throwback to her drama classes at Martin Luther King High School in Atlanta. A good sermon by the pastor about love and forgiveness should prove the perfect antidote for that temper of hers! The nice thing about Gina was that she was never too big to say she was sorry.

Self-assured that he was the victim of their spat, Watkins resumed dialing.

Of the forty or so others on the roster, half weren't in, and the other half already had commitments.

Watkins settled back and studied the facing wall. The evidence of Gina's indictment against him lay there: a slew of team and individual photos, along with plaques, trophies, and mounted bats – testimonials to the life and times of Frederick Alfred Watkins. His playing days had ended about three seasons ago, after opposition players – many of them almost half his age – started calling him the old man.

As he strode out to the wicket to bat, the fielders would say, disparagingly, "Here comes the old man; shouldn't take more than one ball to get him out." And when he surprised them by dispatching the ball to the fence with a quick flash of his willow for an automatic four runs, or over the fence and into the bushes for six, instead of the traditional compliment of "Nice shot," they would ask, pointedly, "How old are you, man? You've got to be pushing at least fifty."

At first, he took the comments as ribbing designed to rattle him into playing rash strokes. But then, he knew he was in the twilight of his career when Pierre started putting him lower and lower in the batting order, and stopped using him as a bowler. Youth, not experience, seemed to be the criterion for selection. Then the captain arbitrarily cut him from the active roster. The first few times Pierre did that, he was diplomatic about it: "We want to rotate the roster, and give some of the newer players a chance." The next match: "We are resting you for the big game." Finally, Pierre really insulted him when he said, "You might hurt yourself."

That really hurt. Sure, at fifty-plus, he was ready to concede that he no longer was the big hitter and prolific scorer he used to be. He didn't see the ball as early and his timing was a bit off. And, yes, he would be the first to admit that when it was his turn to be on the field on defense, he had more than his share of dropped catches, misfields, and wild or feeble throws, and he did take longer to get up when he fell. But he thought he still could stroke the little red ball with his blade with the grace and style lacked by many contemporaries. He honestly believed he still had a few good years left.

But he was a proud man and he wasn't about to belittle himself by begging for a pick. So he simply made it easy on Pierre by showing up for games in his street clothes instead of his whites, signaling to the captain that he didn't expect to play.

Though his playing days were over, his club mates didn't put him entirely out to pasture. They appointed him treasurer, and added the glorified title of manager. The extra title meant that he was the de facto club leader and elder statesman.

As he scrutinized the wall, eyes coming to rest on the nicely framed farewell photo of him in his blazer with the club's badge – a crest of two crossed bats over a ball with the initials FCC in navy blue with white etchings – on the pocket, and a navy-blue tie with thick white stripes, Watkins felt a twinge of excitement, a rush of memories of heroic acts with bat and ball. If ever he wanted to play, today was the perfect opportunity to do so, if only for a few hours.

He estimated that Gina would be back from church by 1:20 p.m. Their daughter, Maggie, her husband, Stephen, and their son, Edward, should arrive from Manhattan around 2:30. If Fernwood batted first, perhaps he could talk Pierre into elevating him in the batting order. That way he could get a good knock before heading home to fire up the grill.

Yes, he'd show his critics today who was the old man!

Watkins made a final call.

The phone rang forever before Harold Richardson "Pops" Minster answered. Like Pierre, Minster was out of breath, and with good reason: He had been out in his backyard garden, turning over the soil.

"We have a game today," Watkins said. "Did you get a chance to repair those bats?"

Pops assured him that the bats had been repaired and oiled and were ready to be picked up.

"I'll be dropping by to pick them up," Watkins said.

One chore left.

Watkins wrote an e-mail to Bhula Marfatia, PhD., chairman, disciplinary committee, New Jersey Cricket League:

Dear Bhula Marfatia, PhD.

As you are aware, Fernwood Cricket Club is scheduled to play Jamaica Rebels at our ground today in the opening game of the season for both clubs.

Let this be a notice to them that any intentional injury to any of Fernwood's players will be reported to the township police.

I sincerely mean this. Let us have some discipline, for heaven's sakes!

Sincerely,

Frederick Alfred Watkins

Watkins pondered how he should sign off, and added *"Manager."*

That, he vowed to himself, would be his last official act as manager.

His cricket clothes and hat weren't in the bottom dresser drawer where he normally stored them. Could it be that they were among the items in the two large garbage bags Gina had donated to the Goodwill Industries thrift store?

Perish the thought! Gina knew that any cricket-related item in the house was sacred. No amount of washing could shrink those memories.

The clothes turned up in a bin in the utility room. Watkins put them in a plastic bag, along with his sneakers, and retrieved his cricket bag from a closet shelf.

The air was heavy with the smell of gasoline and fresh-cut grass as the neighborhood's lawn-mowing marathon entered its second day. Watkins had performed the ritual first thing Saturday, sparing himself an almost certain citation and fine from the township lawn inspector.

Pumped up and whistling in anticipation of another stance at the wicket, and determined to make it a good one, Watkins tossed the steel rake, yard broom and shovel into his Volkswagen station wagon, grateful that Gina wasn't around to see him do so. He automatically was the prime – usually the only – suspect each time a garden tool, folding chair or kitchen utensil went missing. Gina had never forgiven him for the salad bowl that disappeared. The club had given it to her, during one of its annual presentation-of-award ceremonies, for her "Years of Dedicated Service." Gina discovered the bowl missing in the dead of winter. He had no recollection of having taken it to the grounds but, to her, it was a matter of simple deduction: Because nobody would have come to the house and taken it, and because it wouldn't have sprouted legs and walked, he had to have been the culprit, given his history of taking things to the grounds and forgetting them.

Watkins was righting the mailbox when an Eyewitness News TV-8 truck with a satellite dish on the roof rolled into the driveway next door. A bushy-headed, middle-aged man in a Philadelphia Phillies baseball sweatshirt, khaki trousers and Timberland boots alighted.

"How's them Phillies, huh?" Watkins called out.

"How about that!" Michael Hankowsky answered, and proceeded to give him an earful about the Phillies' overnight win against the Cardinals in Philadelphia. "So," he said, at the end of his tale of no-hitters, "when are you going to sign me up for cricket? You did tell me cricket is the granddaddy of baseball and I'm still a halfway decent softball player."

Watkins smiled. His neighbor was being charitable. His comment to Hankowsky that day, six years earlier when his neighbor first saw him in his whites, was that baseball was a bastardized version of cricket. Hankowsky's eyebrows went haywire at the remark, his eyes glowed, and he made vague threats about having him deported to Trinidad. Watkins had been trying to make amends ever since by feigning an interest in baseball.

"If you're really serious, how about today?" Watkins said. "The game starts at 1, so you've got plenty of time."

"All I have to do is transmit some video; then I'm a free man."

Watkins was wary of the glib response. "What about your wife? I'm sure she has a lot of chores around the house for you today."

"Mary?" Hankowsky dismissed the thought with a wave. "Piece of cake. If she makes a fuss, I'll bring her and Timmy along. We'll make a picnic out of it. That's what you said it's like, right?"

"That was back in the old days. You got any white clothes?"

Hankowsky tugged on the off-white sweatshirt. "How about this?"

"No good," Watkins said. "You've got to wear all white – shirt, sweater, trousers, sneakers. The Sports Shoppe at the Echelon Mall has a little cricket section. The prices aren't bad."

"I'll check it out."

A woman in a red silk robe, three-quarter length, and slippers, came out of the house across the cul-de-sac and picked up a newspaper from her lawn. Watkins waved to her.

"You guys wouldn't want to go to a baseball game today, would you?" Carmen Alvarez said. "A doubleheader."

"I pass," Watkins said.

"Good seats."

Mrs. Alvarez sounded like a scalper pedaling tickets outside a Philadelphia sports arena during a playoff game. Watkins didn't envy her. Mrs. Alvarez's latest boyfriend dragged her out to a Phillies game at the start of the season and, beginners' luck, she got hit on the head with a foul ball in Seat No. 59, Row 22, Level 2, at the top of the seventh inning.

Watkins remembered those numbers – 59-22-2-7 – because the Philadelphia Daily News cited them in a story about the incident, and thousands of gamblers played those very numbers in the daily lottery the next day and split two million and change in winnings.

Mrs. Alvarez was knocked out cold and awoke in a hospital bed with more than a dozen business cards of ambulance-chasing lawyers beneath her pillow and taped to her hands. As a public relations gesture, the ball club offered two season tickets for her and her boyfriend for the rest of their "natural lives." She got the tickets and a lot more with the help of one of those ambulance chasers. By now, everyone in the neighborhood had been out to at least one game on her tickets.

"Would love to go," Hankowsky told the poor woman, "but today I venture into the brave new world of cricket. Did Freddie ever tell you we've got a cricket club right here in Fernwood and he's in charge?"

"Was," Watkins said.

"That's what Gina told me," Mrs. Alvarez said. "Got himself written up in the papers and everything."

"I have to run," Watkins said.

Mentally, he put Hankowsky down as a "definite," and wife Mary and son Timmy as additions to the cheerleading squad.

10:22 a.m.

Watkins tuned in to 90.1 FM on his radio dial as he entered Gardenia Drive from Gardenia Court, his cul-de-sac. The anchor of Caribbean Rhythms was giving news briefs of events over the last week in the West Indies, bringing him up-to-date on a region of the world that, although he no longer called it home, part of him refused to let go of. The news was the usual: hurricane damage in Antigua, an earth tremor in St. Vincent, another volcanic eruption in Montserrat, a power struggle involving the two major parties in Trinidad, political violence in Jamaica.

The anchor then kicked off the next half-hour with a medley of pop tunes, arranged in an up-tempo calypso-soul-reggae beat, by the Mighty Sparrow.

Watkins hummed along with the music, head bobbing, as he followed the winding drive through the Cherry

Woods development with its pretentious, single-family homes on spacious lots with blossoming cherry trees. Twenty-five years earlier, when he and Gina, then newly wed, moved from Philadelphia to Fernwood, the township was considered the sticks, best known for its "pick-your-own" strawberry, apple, peach and tomato farms. Today, it was hailed in real estate trade magazines and the media as the most affluent of the new communities that had sprung up seemingly overnight in the outer ring of Cherry Hill, South Jersey's largest suburb of Philadelphia.

Two political campaign posters had sprouted overnight on lawns along the drive.

NO TIME FOR CHANGE – Vote Tuesday June 12 – Neil Quigley for Mayor – said one, with a mug of a man in his late sixties, dark-haired with white sideburns, a stern demeanor and all-seeing eyes.

TIME FOR CHANGE – Vote Tuesday, June 12 – Council-woman Andrea Grimes for Mayor – said the other, with a mug of a middle-aged woman with a Cleopatra hairstyle, equally stern demeanor and all-seeing eyes.

Watkins braked suddenly, then backed up to make room for a tractor-trailer loaded with sod.

The driver made a left turn across his path into Park Lane.

On impulse, Watkins followed the truck.

The lane dead-ended at a parking lot with a sign: *Green Acres, Local Assistance program – This site dedicated to permanent recreational and open space – New Jersey Department of Environmental Protection – No animals, golfing, alcohol or overnight parking permitted.*

The driver parked the rig near a long fence overlooking four baseball-size fields, each encircled by walking paths.

Three of the fields boasted baseball diamonds, bases, mounds and deep-green, freshly laid sod. Sprinkler systems were turned on at those fields, creating a light mist.

The fourth field was half-covered with sod. About a dozen men were playing soccer on the bald spot of that field.

Watkins parked alongside the rig and watched the driver hop out. He wore a green T-shirt with lettering beneath the left pocket that identified him as Tony and his company as Anastasia Landscaping & Irrigation.

Tony leaned over the fence and shouted in Spanish to the soccer players. The men hopped aboard forklifts and drove the equipment toward him.

The rig driver looked his way and said, "You're not from engineering, are you?"

"I'm from the cricket club," Watkins replied. "We've played in this park for twenty-five years."

"Cricket!" Tony screwed up his face as if hit by a foul smell. "What's cricket?"

Seconds into his explanation about wickets and flat bats, Watkins saw Tony's eyes fog up. He quit because it was apparent he was telling Tony more than he wanted to know.

"So, where do you play now?" Tony asked.

"Temporarily, down at the middle school," Watkins said. "We'll be back to play here Sunday, June 10 – that's two days before the elections - following the dedication. Field Number Four, the one you're sodding now, is the old cricket field. That's where we'll be playing."

"Oh, yeah?" Tony drawled. "As far as I know that field also has been assigned to Little League. Then again, what do I know? I'm just the sod man."

The workers arrived in their forklifts. Tony activated a mechanical arm that lifted skids stacked with sod. Watkins started to back out.

"A bit of advice," Tony said, and Watkins stopped the wagon. "Before you make plans to return here, you might want to check with Max Kruger."

"Who's Max Kruger?"

"Who's Max Kruger?" Tony was an echo chamber. "You say you've played cricket here for twenty-five years and you've never crossed swords with Max Kruger!"

"Who's Max Kruger?"

"Little League chief," said Tony. "Thinks he owns the place. Stick around. He'll be here soon telling us how to do our job."

"I deal with Mr. Sarubbi, the township recreation director. He's the one who assigns the fields to the various clubs."

"Well," Tony said, and pulled the lever to lower the suspended skids onto a forklift, "good luck."

Watkins pondered the "good luck" remark, not sure how Tony intended it. Was the landscaper suggesting the cricket club was in danger of losing its field to Little League? He didn't think it possible, not with Sarubbi in its corner.

Gardenia fed into the Boulevard, the major drag into Philadelphia.

The biggest, and some had asserted, the tackiest of the neon signs along the boulevard was for the Sunrise Motel, with its logo of a rising sun and a billboard with flashing, multicolored lights that read: *Truckers Welcomed, $35 for a single, Swimming Pool, Cable-TV, King Bed, Jacuzzi.*

Watkins turned into the entrance to the motel, which consisted of a detached, two-story office building in the front, and two long, single-story, barracks-like buildings in back. The rear buildings faced each other across a courtyard, in the middle of which was a fenced-in swimming pool.

Watkins parked in the office building lot and went in.

A man in a Philadelphia Flyers hockey sweatshirt was speaking across the front counter to a woman, mid-twenties, with plaited hair that snaked all the way down her back. The customer was trying to negotiate an hourly rate, but the clerk wasn't budging on the daily rate. The man gave up and, muttering, forked over thirty-five dollars. The two got into a back-and-forth over the seven percent sales tax. The clerk, sighing, gave up on the tax and shoved a dog-eared registration book across the desktop. The man saw no reason to sign, but the clerk insisted, that it was the law in New Jersey. He scribbled in the book. She handed him a key and he shuffled past.

Only then did the clerk look at him at the other end of the counter. She beamed. "Hi, Watkins."

"Hi, Jayati."

"You want Daddy?" she said.

"Big Daddy," he replied.

Jayati opened a door at the end of the tiny enclosure, admitting Watkins to the foot of the steps to the second level. Watkins climbed to the top.

Raj Bhattacharya, clad in a black cashmere sweater, sat behind a desk in an office at the top of the steps, a phone to his ear. He was an expansive man, late fifties, silver-haired, with craters for cheeks and a matching wide mouth, but with bright, almost twinkling eyes that made up for any facial imperfections.

Bhattacharya hung up, extended a hand that was all meat, and said, "That was Singh."

"Singh?"

"Left-handed Indian fellow. Sikh. Googly bowler. Said he played against Imran Khan during a Pakistan visit to Punjab. I gave him your name and telephone number a few weeks back. He was supposed to get in touch with you."

"No one named Singh called."

"Guess the Sikh's head's too hot right now," said Bhattacharya.

"How come?"

Bhattacharya leaned back. "Know the old gas station down on Route 38, the one where the attendant got killed back in November? It went on the auction block. The Sikh showed up and starts bidding against me. The guy just got off the boat and right away he wants to muscle in on me. I gave him a couple bucks to shut up."

"Sounds like a racket."

"Yeah, but the Sikh wants more than a couple bucks to keep quiet." Bhattacharya gave a little chuckle. "I pulled out of the bidding and he got stuck with the property. Been robbed six times. The last time, he got shot. On top of that, he's making pennies on the dollar at the pump and can't meet his mortgage payments. The guy's so desperate he's talking crazy stuff about putting a match to the place to collect the insurance. I just made him an offer. He's going to think it over and get back to me."

Bhattacharya chuckled louder at the humanitarian gesture that would add to his bottom line.

"Seems every time I come here you're on the phone wheeling and dealing," Watkins said.

"True," Bhattacharya said, chortling. "So, what are you up to these days?"

"I'm newly retired."

"Aw, come on." The tone was one of exaggerated disbelief. "You're too young to retire."

Watkins smiled. That's what he used to tell himself. That was before the ad agency landed a nice casino account, making it an attractive takeover candidate. A bunch of Chicagoans in suits showed a month later, introduced themselves as the new owners, and offered the old-timers a buyout package. He took it.

"Took the buyout, huh?" Bhattacharya leaned farther back, eyes twinkling as they normally did whenever he had a bright idea. "Maybe I can make that lump sum work for you."

"I'm not interested in investing in any gas station, motel, 7-Eleven, or Dunkin' Donuts."

"You're stereotyping me." Bhattacharya pulled a business card out from the desk drawer and handed it to Watkins. It said: *Bhattacharya Enterprises.* "I'm going public. Remember Siddique? Used to play for us. Siddique's an investment banker now. He's preparing a prospectus for my new company. Hope to raise eight, ten million dollars in the initial stock offering. I'll be using the cash to branch out. No more motels, gas stations or convenience stores. I'm taking the Indian entrepreneurial experience to a new level."

"And what level is that, Big Daddy?"

"Everybody likes Indian food, right?" Bhattacharya said. "How about a chain of Indian fast-food restaurants? Head-to-head against McDonald's and Burger King up and down the East Coast?"

"Aren't you worried that you might be spreading yourself too thin?" Watkins asked the question because he knew better than to render an opinion. Maharaj Bhattacharya was a man with no shortage of business ideas – some flew, some were stillborn; most never got beyond the talking stage.

Bhattacharya pulled a glossy color photo of a Cessna from the desk drawer. "Just ordered it," he said, holding up the image. "I'll be flying back and forth visiting my properties. By the way, I'm looking for a pilot. You know how to fly a small plane?"

He said it with a straight face.

"First, you want me to invest in your enterprise, next you want me to be your personal pilot," Watkins said. "All I came here for is to ask you a favor."

"Just say the word."

Watkins told the businessman about the game, and Mrs. Vijay Patel's refusal to let him speak to her husband. Vijay Patel was more than the club's new manager. He also was the team's wicketkeeper, which made him a key player.

"Vijay Patel married!" Bhattacharya was incredulous. "Is that the same Vijay who said he didn't intend to get hitched because Western women were too spoiled and independent?

"That's him."

"The same one who said cricket was his woman, and when he dies he wants to be buried in the middle of the wicket?"

"You have a good memory."

"Holy cow!" Bhattacharya ran his fingers through tousled hair. "Tell me: How did that happen?"

"His parents fixed him up with a bride from New Delhi," Watkins related, reporting back the story as told to him by Vijay Patel. "We kidded him about losing his independence but he swore it would be different with him. He was going to let his bride-to-be know that his only vice was cricket. He would be her slave during the week but that weekends, spring to fall, were his."

"That sounds like Vijay, all right," Bhattacharya said. "He always had a big mouth."

"After he got married, he brought her out to a game, but she kept to herself in the car in the ninety-plus-degree weather, the windows rolled up," Watkins recalled. "He said she was shy, being a princess and an only child."

"A princess, huh? That means he got a big dowry for her," Bhattacharya said.

"He must have. He moved out of The Fernwood Apartments to a mansion on the Westside."

"Married to a princess." Bhattacharya grew pensive. "And from New Delhi. Forget it. He ain't leaving that house. You can scratch him from the lineup."

"That's where you come in," Watkins said.

Bhattacharya again chortled, baring teeth so spaced out that Watkins doubted even braces could bring them together. "What conspiracy would you draw me into?"

"You're still president of the South Jersey chapter of the New Jersey Indian Association, aren't you? I figure if you called and identified yourself as such maybe Mrs. Patel might let you talk to her husband."

Bhattacharya reached for the phone. Watkins gave him the number and Bhattacharya dialed.

Watkins reckoned that Mrs. Patel must have been sitting by the phone, prepared to intercept any further attempts to snare her husband away from her, for she answered the moment Bhattacharya stopped dialing.

He listened, on edge, as Bhattacharya introduced himself as the president of the South Jersey chapter of the New Jersey Indian Association, congratulated Mrs. Patel on he marriage to the highly esteemed Vijay Patel. He invited her to the next association convention at the local Sheraton Hotel where, he assured her, she was sure to meet many people from New Delhi. He then asked for Vijay Patel, put a hand over the mouthpiece, and said to Watkins, "She's gone to get him."

Watkins' spirits rose. Bhattacharya had lost none of his flair for mischief. "I'll talk to him when he gets on," Watkins said.

"I'll handle it," Bhattacharya said, then spoke into the receiver, "Hey, Patel, kya haal hai yaar. Bahut dinse baat nahin hui… Watkins mere saath hai. Abhi baat karna safe hai?"

Watkins shifted uncomfortably in his seat. The Indians and Pakistanis in the club had a habit of doing what Big Daddy just did. In the middle of a conversation in English, they would pull the old switcheroo. He was never sure he wasn't being badmouthed.

"Thought you spoke Bengali," Watkins said, as Bhattacharya hung up. "That sounded like Hindi to me."

"I spent some time in Bombay. You pick up the language."

"What's the deal on Patel?"

"He knew nothing about the game," Bhattacharya said.

"He's about to tell his wife his first big lie: The Indian association has invited him to address its next convention on the contribution of South Asians to the New Jersey economy. Vijay's a state statistician, that's right up his alley. He'll tell her that the association board is meeting in emergency session at 1 o'clock, today at my motel and wants him to come over to discuss his presentation. He doesn't anticipate a problem."

Watkins offered his palm.

Bhattacharya leaned over to slap it. "They have only one car, and he has to leave it for his wife. You're to wait for him on the edge of the trees. You're supposed to be an Indian official come to pick him up. So, whatever you do, don't get out of the car."

Mentally, Watkins put Patel down as another "definite." Snatching him from Mrs. Patel's grasp was a brilliant coup, but he still needed players. He sized up Bhattacharya. "What about you? We could use your bowling today."

"Me!" Bhattacharya laughed. "I haven't played with you guys since my wife ran off with that no-good Mohiuddin." The laughter died and he grew serious. "Bring him into the business and how does he repay me?"

Watkins nodded at Bhattacharya's belly. "You could use the exercise."

"True, true." The Mohiuddin betrayal was quickly forgotten. "Tell you the truth, I was thinking of coming back. But not today."

"It's spring. It's beautiful outside. Perfect day for cricket."

"Yeah, but spring's my busiest season. Come here." Bhattacharya rose, flicked a loose thread off pleated pants, and steered his visitor to the lone window overlooking the front parking lot.

Motorists were pulling in; others were leaving.

"A few years ago, the fear of AIDS drove them off," he said. "Today, AIDS is just another disease, like cancer. You don't hear too much about it anymore. On a day like today, it's like mating season. The rooms turn over two, three times."

"The IRS must really love you."

"The IRS doesn't get to see the books downstairs." Bhattacharya withdrew a ledger from the pile of documents on the desk. "The IRS gets this." He held the ledger up like a championship trophy. "By the way, I've got something for you."

Bhattacharya went into an adjoining room and emerged with two Gray Nichols cricket bats in plastic sleeves. "For the club," he said. "Picked them up in Calcutta last month. Of course, it's all tax-deductible, but that's between me and the IRS."

Watkins thanked him for the bats, and Bhattacharya escorted him downstairs.

A chubby youngster with a virgin moustache and a striking resemblance to Bhattacharya had taken over at the counter. He wore an oversized shirt and baggy jeans, with low pockets.

"You remember my son, don't you?" Bhattacharya said.

"Surajit, right?" Watkins said to the boy. He remembered him as a nine-year-old who was regarded as the next generation that would ensure the survival of the Fernwood Cricket Club far into the twenty-first century. But Surajit, like the other sons of players, had other interests. He would have been fourteen now.

"Mr. Watkins," Surajit said, and they pumped hands.

"How about the boy?" Watkins asked the father. "He was a pretty good fielder."

Bhattacharya spoke what to the untrained ear might have sounded like gibberish and from the boy's smile Watkins could tell Surajit had jumped at the chance to get away from cutting grass and helping his sister clean up after the guests.

"I still have my whites; maybe they'll fit him," Bhattacharya said.

Jayati returned to take over from Surajit behind the counter, and the boy went to get his father's whites.

"Think of what I said about getting that lump sum to work for you," Bhattacharya said as they waited near the wagon for Surajit. "It's not only fast-food. There are lots of distressed properties on the market around here. Now is a good time to buy."

"You sound like a real estate agent."

"True," he said, and Watkins didn't know whether Bhattacharya was referring to the bit about distressed properties or the fact that he sounded like a real estate broker. "So, what do you do with your spare time?"

"I'm writing a novel," Watkins said. "Murder mystery."

Bhattacharya's eyes widened. "How about that! A book writer, huh? Am I in it?"

"You'll have to buy the novel to find out."

"I could give you lots of stories," Bhattacharya said. "These rooms are full of them…. Everything's okay at home?"

"Gina's fine." Watkins swallowed. She should be fine by now, he told himself. "She keeps herself busy by doing a little volunteer work at Our Lady of Lourdes Hospital in Camden. We have a grandson. Entering the terrible two's. My daughter's bringing him down later today from Manhattan. I plan to be back home in time to fire up the grill."

Bhattacharya was right about the whites. They fit Surajit perfectly.

******

Minutes later, Watkins pulled into the no-name, independent gas station on Route 38 and waited with his plastic for the attendant to emerge from the six-foot-by-six foot office between two rows of pumps.

Nothing stirred. The lights inside the enclosure were on, despite the strong sunlight. Watkins' antenna went up. According to the news reports in November, a motorist checked out the enclosure after no one appeared to serve him and found the overnight attendant slumped to the floor with a bullet wound to the head.

This morning, though, a live person was there. Surajit caught sight of him first.

"Do you see him?"

Watkins looked in vain. "Where?"

"Behind the cigarettes."

Something, or someone, moved behind the rows of Marlboro cigarettes and quarts of oil that lined the see-through sheet plastic. Watkins made out the purple turban, the face below the turban, then the staring eyes.

A door was pushed open gradually and out came a heavily bearded, turbaned figure in greasy navy blue work clothes. He came straight toward them, brown face shiny, eyes glaring and focused, clutching a large cricket bat, a giant bulldog at his heels.

"Mid-grade," Watkins said, the engine still running, ready to drive off should the attendant wield that bat.

"You want fill up?" the attendant asked in a clipped accent.

"Fill up," Watkins said.

The attendant unscrewed the gas cap, and shoved the nozzle in, using the same hand, suspicious eyes never leaving Watkins, still clutching the bat.

"You play cricket?" Watkins asked.

The attendant's eyes registered surprise and in that moment he looked more like mid-twenties than late forties. "You know cricket?"

"I'm from Trinidad," Watkins said. "Surajit here was born in America, but his parents are from India via Kenya."

"Your name's not Watkins, is it?"

"Freddie Watkins."

"Ahhhh," the attendant sang. His eyes got brighter and he smiled, exposing a gold tooth in his upper jaw. "Raj Bhattacharya was telling me about you."

"You're Singh, right?"

"Bhupinder Singh."

"Just left Raj's place," Watkins said. "He said you played cricket back home."

"You know Imran Khan?"

Watkins nodded. "One of the world's greatest. Married that English girl. Jewish. He ran for president of Pakistan. His critics said his marriage was part of a Jewish conspiracy to control the Muslims in Pakistan. He lost."

"I played against Imran back in Punjab," Singh said.

"You still play?"

"Not since I come to America."

Watkins pointed to the bat. "I see you still carry around your willow."

Singh held up the bat, no longer in a threatening manner, but as an instrument of pride. "I brought it to America in case I find cricket. But here at the station, I use it for protection."

"Rough neighborhood, huh?"

"Very rough." Singh unbuttoned his shirt to display what Watkins assumed was a bulletproof vest. "I also wear this." He tapped the black garment with his knuckles. "Got shot in the chest."

"How did it happen?"

Singh's story sounded familiar: An electrical engineer by trade, he had arrived in the United States a year earlier but had been unable to find work in his field. Pumping gas was the only way to make a buck. Late one night, less than a month after he bought the station, two masked men jumped out of a beat-up Chevy, flashed handguns and ordered him back into the enclosure.

"They didn't want cash," Singh said. "Just the cigarettes."

"They robbed you for your cigarettes?"

"Marlboros," Singh said. "They wanted only the Marlboros. Then shot me." Singh withdrew the nozzle, screwed the cap back on, and returned the nozzle to the pump. He took the plastic, went into his office and returned with a clipboard, minus the cricket bat, but with the bulldog still at his heels. "Do you know a good lawyer?"

"Sure," Watkins signed the attached receipt. "His name is Emile Pierre. He's captain of our cricket team. Surajit and I are on the way to our season opener. We're short. We could use a good batsman and googly bowler."

"I bowl, I bat," Singh said with a shrug, "but I might be a bit rusty."

"It should only take a game or two to bring back your form." Watkins was impressed by Singh's modesty. Most newcomers to the club boast about being adept with the bat and the ball, but nine out of ten times it's all in their heads.

He gave Singh directions to the grounds.

"Maybe I come by later," Singh said.

"Tell me something," Watkins said. "If the robbers shot you, why do you need a lawyer?"

"The robbers shot me, and I get arrested. Is that justice? Tell me, is that justice?"

"Why arrest you?"

"It's a long story," he said. "I come by maybe later. I talk to your lawyer."

As he drove off, Watkins caught a glimpse of Bhupinder Singh in the rearview mirror headed back to his plastic office, bulldog at his heels.

He put the Sikh down, mentally, as a maybe.

Back in residential Fernwood, Watkins turned into Lost Tree Drive, the main road through the Westside, continued past the Meadows and the Manors, both walled communities of fantasy homes with private security guards, and into the narrower Hidden Acres Lane.

The name V. Patel was on the third, freestanding mailbox along the forested lane.

Watkins turned into the dirt driveway at the mailbox, and followed deep tire marks in the still soggy earth. Birds twittered. A squirrel darted across the path and up a tree.

"Wow!" Surajit exclaimed. "And I thought our house was big."

The object of the boy's wonder was a three-story white mansion in the middle of a clearing in the woods another hundred yards or so ahead. The sounds of nature gave way to human voices and a low, mechanical purr. Two men were laying sod at the front and back of the mansion. A flatbed truck with sod was being driven from the front to the side of the house. A small woman in a sari and a stout Indian man stood in the front, arched doorway. Vijay Patel wore a gray business suit and red tie and carried a large briefcase.

As instructed, Watkins waited with his passenger on the edge of the property. From this distance he doubted that Mrs. Patel could tell he wasn't Indian. Patel said something to Mrs. Patel and she went back into the house. Patel came toward them, sporting a devilish grin.

"You look as though you're on your way to a convention," Watkins said as Patel climbed into the backseat.

"Sorry, man, but I never got your message."

"I assume you have your whites in that briefcase," Watkins said.

"Along with my sneakers." Patel laughed so hard the car vibrated. "From now on, any correspondence or messages should be directed to my office in Trenton."

Watkins felt a sense of triumph in having snared Patel away to help salvage the game. The next step was to get Patel to accept his responsibility as new manager. That was key if he was to keep his promise to Gina to give up the sport. Patel would just have to find a way to get around his wife. Sounded heartless, but that was the reality. If Patel couldn't handle it, he should be man enough to say so.

Patel must have read his thoughts, for he said, "I told the wife I'll be working overtime on weekends until September. She comes from a family of business people. She understands the concept of making money."

Sounded good, Watkins thought, but he saw a flaw: "That means she'll be expecting to see something extra in your paycheck each week."

"I've got a simple answer for that: I plan to take time off in lieu of overtime pay," Patel replied.

"And what happens when the time comes to take time off?"

"I'll send her back home for a long visit," Patel said. "When she returns, I'll tell her I took the time off while she was away to do some work around the house." He laughed until the tears came.

"Sounds as though you really thought it through," Watkins said.

"I have," Patel bragged, wiping the tears with the back of his hand. "It's foolproof."

Watkins poked Surajit in the side with his elbow. "I hope you're learning."

Surajit smiled. It would be his turn one day.

"One more stop," Watkins said.

******

Harold Richardson "Pops" Minster lived in The Village, the so-called "old section" of Fernwood, a maze of asphalt-paved roads with no curbs or sidewalks and one-of- a-kind, modest homes on irregular-shaped lots.

Watkins' destination was a rancher with a carport on a well-tended lot. He pulled up in the driveway behind Pops' pickup truck.

An Anchor Fence Company van was parked in the driveway next door. Two men were unloading lumber from the van.

"Didn't realize you had black neighbors," one of the truckers said.

"They ain't black; they're Jamaicans," the other man replied.

Watkins told himself he had to remember that one.

Stepping out of the wagon, he spotted Pops in his back-yard garden, dressed in a nylon warm-up suit and pushing a rototiller. He also spotted the canvas cricket bag on a picnic table on the edge of the garden. A cricket ball dangled mid-air on the end of a string tied to the branch of a shade tree.

Watkins checked out the bag on the table. The intoxicating smell of linseed oil hit him the moment he unzipped it. He sniffed the bats, and ran his fingers over the new rubber that encased the handles and the fresh twine that encircled the flat surfaces.

Pops shut down his machine and ambled over. Sweat trickled down the cracks of his face and the cleft in his chin onto his clothes.

"See you've got new neighbors," Watkins said.

"They moved in last month." Pops fumbled through the dirty work clothes for cigarettes. "From South Philly. They probably asked for their money back when they found out I ain't Italian. Now, they're putting up a fence."

"Maybe it's time you moved," Watkins said.

"Yeah, there goes the neighborhood."

"Where's the wife?"

"Her pastor croaked." Pops lit up. "She went down to the church to help with the funeral arrangements."

To the newer members of the Fernwood Cricket Club, he was simply Pops, a grandfatherly figure who brought food to the grounds midway through the games, then sat off to the side on a lawn chair, quietly chain-smoking and imbibing himself with white rum from his native Jamaica. By the end of the game, he would stagger to his car but would insist on driving himself home. He had run off the road a few times, but never hit anything more serious than an unattended lemonade stand.

Watkins looked at Pops now and saw something more than the club's cook: he saw its founder, first captain, first president, first everything, including first nonwhite resident of Fernwood, according to the U.S. census. More important, he saw another prospect in his desperate effort to put a team together.

"If you came with us, you might be able to get a knock today," he said.

Minster straightened up, as if pricked in the back. "What are you saying, man?"

"We might be short today," Watkins said. "Go get your whites."

Pops' body shook with excitement.

"Don't go 'way," he said, and ran for the back door.

Watkins smiled at the hop-along movement. The problem with people like Pops was that they didn't know when it was time to hang it up for good. He got the message a long time ago. Sure, he wasn't ready but didn't fight it, either. Pops was sixty-four, a year shy of full Social Security benefits, and was more of a liability than an asset on the field, but he empathized with the man. Pops' cricketing career had ended just as abruptly, and unceremoniously, as his. One day you're a superstar, the next you get no respect. If today could be his last hurrah, why not Pops'?

As they awaited his return, Watkins selected a bat from the bag and warmed up by hitting the ball that dangled in midair. He tried a different stroke each time the ball swung back his way, feeling the excitement building inside. Yes, he would show them today who's the old man!

Patel ran up. "Trouble!"

Watkins looked past him at a four-door Lincoln Continental that had rolled to a stop behind his wagon. An African-American woman, topped by a big, black hat and a black coat that reached to her ankles, got out.

Damn, Watkins thought. "Good morning, Mrs. Minster."

Wilhelmina Minster responded with a glare as she crossed the lawn for the front door.

"Here we go again," Patel said.

Watkins tossed the cricket gear into the back of the wagon and hurried with Patel into the vehicle. He turned on the engine.

Mrs. Minster's voice sounded the moment she entered the house: "Where do you think you're going?"

No answer.

"Don't tell me you're going to play cricket with that man?"

Pops held his fire.

"That man already has turned you into a heathen, and now he's about to break up your marriage."

Still, no answer.

The front door flew open and Pops came out in a white hat, V-neck sweater and trousers. In one hand, he carried a large canvas kit with the handle of a cricket bat sticking out, and, in the other, a grocery bag.

Mrs. Minster appeared on the front steps. "Harold, you come back here this minute!"

Patel had opened a door. Pops threw the kit and bag in and climbed in after them.

"Drive!" Pops commanded.

"Perhaps this isn't such a good idea," Watkins said. He felt a sudden queasiness. They had pulled a fast one on Mrs. Patel but had been caught in the act by Pops' wife. There would be repercussions for Pops. "We don't want to break up your marriage."

"What marriage!" Pops said. "Drive!"

Mrs. Minster had advanced across a flowerbed onto the lawn. "Are you defying me, Harold Richardson Minster? Are you?"

"Come on, let's get out of here," Patel said.

About fifty feet away, Mrs. Minster began charging toward them.

Watkins reversed hard, accidentally knocking the Lincoln Continental back down the driveway, and creating enough space between the car and Pops' pickup truck to make a sharp U-turn through the front lawn. Mrs. Minster picked up an object and hurled it in their direction. Watkins heard a loud bang over his head.

"Heathens!" Mrs. Minster shrieked. "Headed straight for hell!"

Pops leaned out the window. "I'll return from hell and take you back with me!" he shouted.

Watkins stopped the wagon a country block away, inspected the roof and saw a dent and sharp scratch near the front on the driver's side. The rear bumper was twisted.

Pops offered to pay for the roof damage. He told Pops to forget it.

Patel opened the grocery bag. No surprise; it was half filled with beef patties.

"Was going to bring them by later," Pops said.

"I can tell you made them," Patel said.

"Smells good, huh?" Pops said.

"By the sizes; big, small and in-between" Patel said. He selected a big one and told the boy, "Don't tell my wife I eat beef when I'm with the guys."

They all laughed.

Watkins also grabbed a big one.

Pops reached into a pocket, pulled out a flask of imported, unlabeled, no-brand Jamaican white rum, unscrewed the cap.

"Isn't it too early to be hitting the sauce?" Patel said.

"It's never too early." He took a swig. "One more year. As soon as I sign up for Social Security, me gone."

"Me gone?" Patel said, mouth full of food.

"Yes, me gone," Pops said. "Way, way, Down Under. The government could send my Social Security checks there."

"Why Australia, Pops?" Patel asked.

"Got a twin brother there," Pops said. "Went over as a trainer in the West Indies team in the '80s. He liked it and stayed."

"You consulted with the wife about that, Pops?" Patel asked.

"Heck, no!"

"When do you intend to tell her?" Watkins said, joining the tease. He had relaxed a bit.

"Never!"

"She'll try to get the government to stop your checks," Patel said.

"Just let her try!" Pops said, and took another swig.

******

It was a ten-minute drive from Pops' place to the George Washington Middle School, tucked away in the woods at the bottom of School House Lane. The parking lot between the school and the school grounds was deserted. Watkins saw a pickup truck in the middle of the ground and a man in white clothes pushing a heavy roller back and forth near the pickup.

"At least our captain's here," Watkins said. "The others are likely to show up when we're through fixing the wicket."

"I also don't see any sign of the Jamaica Rebels," Patel said.

"Hopefully, they got lost," Watkins said.

"No such luck," Pops said, pointing to a caravan of cars and vans beyond the trees.

The caravan turned off the highway into School House Lane and raced toward them. The Jamaica Rebels had arrived in typical Jamaican style, with their usual entourage of about two hundred supporters, reggae music blasting. The vehicles converged on the lot like swarming locusts, filling it and the approaches.

Victor Stuart stood out among the players who emerged from the vehicles, a tall, wiry figure. Stuart turned his face skyward, breathed deeply, and stretched.

Watkins hesitated, then cautiously approached the Jamaica Rebels captain. "Glad to see you made it."

"You got a team?" Stuart didn't ask. He demanded.

"We've got a team," Watkins said.

"Good," Stuart replied. "Tell your players to put on their helmets so we can proceed with your decapitation and get the hell outta here."

12:30 p.m.

In his long association with the sport in America, Frederick A. Watkins had never missed an opportunity to promote cricket as a gentlemen's game. That was how he remembered it on the island. He was taught as a youngster that cricket was more than a game. It was the quintessential sport that helped build character.

But these Jamaicans who called themselves Jamaica Rebels apparently had forgotten their lessons. Or perhaps they never learned them. Why else would they drive more than sixty miles down the Turnpike from urban Newark to his turf in suburban Fernwood to make trifle of his team?

Talk about class!

Calming himself, Watkins retrieved the rake, broom and shovel from the wagon. His teammates relieved him of the tools and proceeded toward Emile Pierre in the middle of the grounds.

Watkins started to follow, thought the pounding music a bit much, and asked Stuart. "Mind lowering the volume?"

46

Stuart turned to a teammate standing outside the van from which the music blared. "Hear that, Selwyn? Old man Watkins don't like reggae music. Wants us to turn the volume down. It might offend his hoity-toity neighbors in their pricey homes."

"No shit." Selwyn reached into the vehicle and turned up the volume. "How's that, old man?"

Watkins let it go. He should have known better.

"Hey!" someone shouted at his back. The man who approached was a short, squat, cross-eyed fellow in a white lab coat. "You Watkins?"

"Depends on who wants to know." The man didn't look like someone from a law firm sent by Gina to serve him with divorce papers, but he wasn't about to take chances.

The stranger introduced himself as Ramjohn Beharry, and said he was sent by the league to umpire the game. "Are you the one I see about getting paid?"

"We usually pay the umpire after the game," Watkins said.

Beharry withdrew a New Jersey Cricket League rulebook from the lab coat. "Umpire fees to be paid upfront," he said, summarizing a paragraph that was highlighted with a yellow marker. "Each team pays me sixty dollars."

Watkins was suspicious. "I thought it was fifty."

"That was last year." His Guyanese accent was unmistakable. "The price gone up." Beharry pointed to another paragraph. The first "f" in the word fifty had been changed to "s" and the second "f" changed to "x" so that "fifty" became "sixty."

"How come the changes are penciled in?" Watkins asked.

"What trouble is this!" Beharry huffed, and stuffed the book into the coat. "You guys got to be making at least a hundred grand apiece to live in a town like this, so what's sixty bucks to you?"

Watkins wasn't about to create a scene. It would be easy enough to find out whether Beharry was on the up-and-up. "I'll get my checkbook in the car."

"Uh-uh." Beharry waved a finger. "No checks."

"Our checks are good."

"No checks." Beharry again pointed to the rulebook.

"He wants no paper trail for the IRS," Stuart said behind them.

Watkins found enough cash on him to pay the umpire. Beharry licked his right thumb and index finger and counted. He held up each bill to the light, scrutinizing the face and back with the intensity of a forgery expert. Satisfied, he lined the bills up, raised an end of the lab coat, revealing a New York Knicks basketball sweatshirt that half-covered a rounded, hairy gut, and pants that had slid off the belly to his crotch. He shoved the money into a back pocket, and consulted his watch.

"It's now 12:35 p.m.," Beharry said. "I want both teams out in the middle at 12:55 so I can read the riot act."

Watkins joined his teammates at the wicket.

Pierre, a wavy-haired, well-toned man, had paused for a breather. Patel had taken over pushing the heavy roller back and forth along the sixty-six-foot-long clay wicket. Pops and Surajit had made themselves useful raking and sweeping the clay ahead of the roller.

"There were cleat marks all over the wicket," Pierre said. "The baseball people must have been using the field."

"Unfortunately, until we get our grounds back in the park, we'll have to share this field with Little League," Watkins said. "That's the word from the recreation director."

Watkins gave the captain a rundown on the people he had called and messages left. With luck, they should have an eleven by game time.

"I also made a few calls," Pierre said. "International Cricket Club in Philly doesn't have a game today. Some of their players might come over."

Pierre grabbed a hammer and a bunch of stakes with attached flags from the back of the pickup and handed them to Watkins. "You mind?"

Watkins didn't protest. He told himself that he could use the exercise.

By the time he was through circling the field, he had worked up a good sweat, putting up the flags to mark the football-field size playing area.

That task completed, he assisted his club mates in lifting the carpet from the back of the truck and rolling it over the smoothed clay. They nailed down the edges of the carpet to the wicket and planted a set of three wooden, knee-high sticks at each end.

Preparation of the wicket completed, Pierre drove the truck toward the bleachers that served as Fernwood's makeshift dugout. Pops sat in the back of the truck like a kid on a hayride, lighting up. Patel and Surajit brought in the rake, broom, shovel, can of extra nails and the hammer. Watkins followed, pushing the roller. Patel, seeing him falling farther and farther behind, asked Watkins whether he wanted to switch chores.

"I'm fine," Watkins puffed.

Jamaica Rebels supporters, many in colorful umbrella hats, were trekking from the parking lot to the bleachers on the opposite side of the field. They lugged folding chairs, blankets, coolers, and boom boxes.

Pierre sat on the aluminum bleachers, scorebook in hand.

"Looks like we're about to get TV coverage," Patel said.

An Eyewitness News TV-8 van had appeared in the lot. A white man in whites alighted from the van.

"Oh, that's just my neighbor, Michael Hankowsky," Watkins said. "I invited him to the game."

"Can he play?" Pierre said.

"We'll soon find out," Watkins said.

Hankowsky surveyed the territory like a motorist who had made a wrong turn and didn't know whether the natives were friend or foe. He appeared relieved when he saw Watkins approaching.

"Tell me how I look," Hankowsky said, with a grin normally reserved for whenever they caught "a big one" during their fishing trips off Barnegat Bay.

"Sharp," Watkins said. That was the truth. "I see you even bought yourself a hat." He couldn't bring himself to tell his neighbor that the hat was more suited for watching cricket in the sun than playing in the field.

"I've bought me more than a hat." Hankowsky shoved open a side door of the van and Watkins saw a large cricket bag sandwiched between two TV monitors and coils of wire and a cooler. Hankowsky opened the bag to reveal a long-handled bat, a pair of batting gloves, and pads for his feet, thighs, waist and arms. At the bottom of the bag was a booklet, *The Rules of Cricket*, and a voluminous book, *History of West Indian Cricket*, by Michael Manley, the late Jamaican prime minister and cricket enthusiast.

"I got a little carried away." Hankowsky hitched the pair of loose-fitting trousers and retied the string that held them up.

"You didn't have to buy all this stuff. The club has plenty of gear."

"The guy at the store said serious cricketers prefer to use their own gear," Hankowsky said. "Look at this mother." Hankowsky took the plastic sleeve off the oversized bat and kissed the flat surface.

Watkins recognized it as a top-of-the-line willow, and thought it akin to putting a Rolls Royce in the hands of a student driver. He imagined that a sucker like Hankowsky came along once in a blue moon, offering the owner a chance to clear his inventory of expensive, slow-moving items. He would have to talk to the dealer.

"Here, I've got something for you." It was a personal check, made out to the Fernwood Cricket Club. Hankowsky had signed it, but left the amount blank. "Dues. You can fill in the amount."

Watkins couldn't bring himself to accept.

"I'm no freeloader," Hankowsky said, and shoved the check into Watkins' pocket. "And I'm in for the long haul."

A black Volkswagen Beetle rolled to a stop behind the TV van and a young man in a Rugters Scarlet Knights basketball sweat suit jumped out.

"Here's Timmy," Hankowsky said. "Couldn't swing it with the wife. Mary said she'd come only if Gina was coming. Is she?"

"Not this time." Watkins turned his attention to the boy. "Where are your whites, Timmy?"

"He's here to film the game for me," Hankowsky said. "I'm thinking maybe I can give you a plug on TV-8 sports roundup tonight."

Timmy went to work, retrieving the camera from his dad's van, hefting it onto his shoulder, and panning the scene.

Watkins escorted his neighbor to the Fernwood bleachers.

Fully introduced, Hankowsky crossed the field with his high-end bat to the opposite bleachers where Timmy was filming the Jamaica Rebels as they went through an exercise and fancy-catching routine, while their supporters settled down to some serious domino-board games.

Watkins peered over Pierre's shoulder as the Fernwood captain wrote down the lineup, beginning with himself, followed by Patel, and Surajit.

A stranger came up and introduced himself as Jamie Cumberbatch from Trinidad. He said he was sent by the International Cricket Club in Philadelphia.

"They said you need players," Cumberbatch added.

"Do you bat, or bowl?" Watkins asked. He knew most of the Philadelphia players. This sprightly, handsome twenty-something, who reminded him of himself eons ago, wasn't one of them.

"I'm a damn good all-rounder – bowling, batting and fielding," Cumberbatch said.

Watkins thought his immodesty was as striking as Bhupinder Singh's modesty.

Pierre put Cumberbatch down, untried, and looked across the field. Timmy had put his camera down, and he and his dad had a little game going. Hankowsky assumed a baseball stance, with the bat straight out instead of pointed to the ground. Timmy under-handed a softball and Hankowsky swatted it way, way back.

A fat boy ran out from the yard of a mansion on the edge of the trees, caught it with a baseball glove and took a spill. The boy got up and tossed the ball back.

"Not bad," Pierre said, and added Hankowsky's name to the batting lineup.

Watkins ambled over to give Hankowsky the good news that he had made the team, that Pierre liked the way he batted.

"Hear that, Timmy?" Hankowsky crowed to his son. "The old man's still got it. Maybe I end up MVP."

"What about me?" the fat boy asked. He was about twelve, with black hair dyed blond, in an oversized shirt that said FUBU.

"What's your name, kid?" Watkins asked.

"Moses."

"Maybe you can be our twelfth man, Moses," Watkins told the boy. "You'll be a regular Gunga Din."

"A who?"

"The water boy," Watkins said. "And if somebody gets hurt, you sub for him."

"You mean I have to wish for somebody to break a leg to get to play?" said Moses.

"That's not nice," Hankowsky scolded him, and whacked another Timmy delivery even farther back.

Watkins returned to the bleachers and let Pierre know that Moses was available, if they got desperate. Pierre didn't answer.

"Here comes Shane Asquith," Patel said.

A white couple with two teenage girls emerged from the crowd in the lot. Asquith was in his whites and carried cricket bag. Wife Cindy and "the girls" tagged along in matching sweatshirts and jeans.

Pierre added the bespectacled Englishman to the lineup.

Beharry hailed out that it was time for the two teams to gather at the wicket for his "riot act" and the coin toss.

Pierre closed the scorebook with no further additions to the lineup. Watkins told himself there was no reason for him to be disappointed at not being included on the team. He hadn't told Pierre he was available. If he didn't get a pick, no big deal. Besides, he needed to get back home soon.

Pierre signaled the approaching Asquiths to join them at the wicket. He shouted to Hankowsky, and waved him over. Timmy walked backward, camera trained on his father as Hankowsky joined them in the middle.

After renewing acquaintances with the Asquiths and introducing them to the newcomers, Fernwood players lined up across the carpet from the opposition. The Jamaica Rebels had a full eleven; Fernwood had the six whose names Pierre had jotted down. Watkins stood aside with Pops, Asquith's ever-smiling American wife, Cindy, and their daughters, plus Moses, who had ambled over, curious as to what it was all about.

"Is *this* your team?" Stuart sneered at Pierre.

Watkins viewed the lineups and couldn't fault Stuart's contemptuousness. Fernwood did look a sorry bunch compared with the Jamaica Rebels. The visitors were a homogeneous team, comprised mostly of ex-professional and semi-professional Jamaican cricket players who lived in the northern part of the state in the New York metropolitan area. They were all urban, gritty players who were on their way to yet another championship last season when they were derailed by the hapless Fernwood, a team that knew how to win only on paper. And, as Gina had deduced accurately, today they were out to exact vengeance.

Pierre said, "We'll have an eleven before start of play."

"Don't expect us to show you any mercy," Stuart said.

"Cricket's a funny game," Pierre reminded him. "The strongest team doesn't always win."

Stuart started to respond in a disparaging way, but Beharry cut him off: "First thing you should know about me is that I don't scare easy." Beharry walked with measured steps between the two lineups. "You see me, you see little, cross-eyed man, someone you figure you could push around. But I come from Guyana and Guyanese people don't tolerate anybody cussing their mothers or their sisters."

He paused, looked around, and getting no challenge, resumed his General Patton-like pacing.

"That's another way of telling you if you don't like my decision, too bad," Beharry continued. "You could scream, you could holler, you could prance all you want, don't waste your breath. If you persist in trying to intimidate me, or curse my mother or my sister, you only get me vex. And when Ramjohn Beharry gets vex, he get damn vex. Is everyone understanding me?"

Beharry's eyes swept the lines. No one challenged him.

"The second thing you should know about Ramjohn Beharry is that he play fair," the umpire went on. "Ask the whole league about me, and they'll tell you that I am the only league umpire who know what he doing. Some guys they send them out to umpire games, they never read this." He waved a book above his head.

Watkins caught the title: *The Laws of Cricket, Second Edition, 1992, Marylebone Cricket Club, London, England.*

"So, if I say a man out, he out," Beharry said. "If I say he ain't out, he ain't out. End of story." Beharry slashed his hand horizontally, a movie director signaling cut. "I always have to remind players, they get spoil watching American sports. Cricket may look like baseball, but it ain't baseball. You don't go charging at anybody with a bat. You don't spit in people's faces. No cussing. No bench-clearing brawls. No questioning the umpire's decision. It just ain't cricket to question the umpire's call. This is a gentlemen's game, so let's behave like gentlemen. Now, before I toss the coin, I want everybody to shake hands. You play fair, you play square."

Watkins looked on passively as the players shook hands. They then formed a circle around Beharry for the coin toss.

"Heads," said Pierre.

"Heads," Stuart said.

"There's only one head," Beharry lectured Pierre. "Somebody got to have tails."

"Heads," said Stuart.

"Then you got tails," Beharry told Pierre, and flipped the coin. The quarter dropped on the edge of the carpet, staggered and fell over the edge. "Heads," Beharry announced, swooping up the coin.

"We bat first," Stuart decided.

Asquith reached over and grabbed Beharry's fist. "Not so fast, old chap. May I see that coin?"

Beharry glared at the Englishman. "You not impugning my integrity, are you?"

Asquith said, "I saw two heads."

"I think it's your glasses," Beharry said. "Them rimless glasses making you see double."

Asquith held Beharry's fist with both hands and tried to pry the fingers loose, but they tightened.

"I don't like that." Beharry jerked the hand away, and shoved it into the lab coat. "I just don't like what you accusing me of. You English people just can't stand being beaten by the colonies."

"Show us the coin," Pierre challenged Beharry. "If it's not a two-headed coin, we'll all apologize."

Beharry fumbled around in his pocket, and produced a coin. "Here!"

Asquith examined the coin. "This isn't it. The coin you tossed wasn't as shiny." He passed it to Pierre, who passed it to Patel and it went from hand to hand. "Let's see what else you've got in that pocket."

"You not calling me a liar, are you?" Beharry said to Asquith.

"You're a bloody cheat," Asquith blurted out.

"That's it!" Beharry said, clearing a path through the Jamaica Rebels, and stomping off. "See you later. Goodbye."

Patel turned to Watkins. "You didn't pay him, did you?"

"I did," Watkins said.

"Never pay an umpire first," Patel said.

Stuart said, "Don't worry, fellers. He's not going anywhere. Hey, Beharry, git your ass back here!"

Beharry came back, raising both hands in the air. "Go on," he invited the Englishman. "Search the pockets. Both of them."

Asquith accepted the invitation, and came up with a regular quarter.

"I apologize," Asquith said.

"Apology accepted," Beharry said. "Let's get on with the game. And no more of this foolishness. And you," he added, pointing to Asquith, "get them rimless glasses checked."

Back at Fernwood's bleachers, Pierre curled up with the scorebook in hand. "Where's Pops?"

Harold Richardson Minster was behind the bleachers taking a swig of white rum. Pierre put his name down.

A bearded man of Indian descent came toward them from the parking lot. He wore white and carried a cricket bat.

"The shrink is here," Patel announced.

Pierre put down Harry Sankar, the Trinidad native and psychologist, as Batsman No. 8, and looked around for three more prospects. "Where's that Moses? I liked the way he dived to take that catch."

"He was wearing a glove," Patel pointed out.

Pierre said, "With Jamaica Rebels batting first, we're likely to be doing a lot of leather-hunting today. We need people with young legs to chase the ball."

Watkins immediately regretted his recommendation, but tried not to show it when he located and gave Moses the good news.

The kid's eyes lit up. "What do I do?"

"They'll teach you as they go along," Watkins said.

Pierre studied the lineup and did a head count. "Two more."

"What about Watkins?" Patel said.

"You don't have to." Watkins tried to be nonchalant about it. "I promised Gina I'd be home once I was through putting a team together."

Pierre sized up Watkins. "I assume you brought your whites. Go put them on."

Ah, spring, Watkins mused, standing now alongside his wagon in the parking lot, trading his street clothes for his whites, then kissing the flat surface of his prized bat. To experience once again the thrill of stroking the little red ball with his willow in this, the world's quint-essential game – granddaddy of American baseball, a pastime rooted in gentlemanly conduct. It was, indeed, a nice day for cricket.

Fitzroy Chong materialized out of nowhere, bat cradled beneath his arm.

"Sorry about being late," the Black Chinaman said to Pierre. "Just got the message from my brother about the game."

Pierre put the lazy Barbadian down in the eleventh and final spot. "All we need now is a scorer."

Cindy Asquith put up a hand. Pierre handed her the scorebook and introduced her to the Jamaica Rebels' scorer, who had come over with his team's scorebook. The scorers sat at a table Pierre set up for them.

After volunteering for the job, Cindy suddenly had reservations about the task at hand. Watkins advised her to write down in Fernwood's book whatever the Jamaica Rebels' scorer wrote in his book.

"But how do I know if he's cheating?" Cindy asked.

"Cheating?" Watkins reacted with feigned shock. "Cindy, you should know by now that there's no such thing in cricket."

Pierre brought his players together, gave the usual pep talk about wanting one hundred percent from everyone, and led the team out.

As his teammates took up positions around the wicket, Watkins asked, "Where do you want me, Skip?"

Pierre scanned the field and said, "Drop back to third man."

Watkins hesitated. He had been playing the game since his formative years on the island but had never pretended to know everything. The deep centerfield positions like long-on and long-off were no problem. Nor were the close-to-the bat positions like silly mid-on, silly mid-off, slips, fine leg, and the midfield positions like square leg, cover, and extra cover.

But when it came to such obscure stuff like backward-square leg, point, and third man, it was all Greek to him. Team captains, acutely aware of that puzzlement among most players, typically would set the field by pointing, "You, over there," and "You, over here." The wannabe-pros like Pierre always tried to show off their book knowledge by telling rather than pointing.

Not wanting to display his ignorance, Watkins headed for a gap in the field placement. Pierre directed Hankowsky to short third man. Watkins saw the mystified look on his neighbor's face and suggested to Hankowsky that he position himself in the gap ten feet or so from him.

Hankowsky moved to the position and was even more mystified. "Why are we fielding behind the catcher?"

"You mean the wicketkeeper," Watkins said, nodding at Vijay Patel, who had taken up duties, with gloves and pads, behind one set of the sticks. "You see, my friend, unlike baseball, the entire field is fair territory. That's why the wicket is in the middle of the field. You and I are back here to catch the balls that are fouled back. If we catch them on the fly before they hit the ground, that's one of the outs."

Umpire Beharry drew Pierre's attention to the dress code and pointed out that Moses, in his FUBU top, was in violation. Pierre trotted off the field and returned with a sweater to cover the offending walking billboard. The sweater hugged Moses' upper body tightly, but hung down to his calves, provoking laughter all around.

Jamaica Rebels spectators applauded as their two opening batsmen came onto the field from their bleachers. Stuart and his batting partner, Long Man, swaggered toward the wicket in their foot pads and heavy gloves, dragging their bats in what Watkins considered a very unprofessional manner. They hadn't seen the need to wear helmets.

"Lash them," shouted a bald-headed, white-bearded man from the Jamaica Rebels' camp.

Watkins joined his teammates in applauding.

Hankowsky asked, "Why are we clapping?"

"Tradition, my friend, tradition," Watkins said. "You wish the opposition's batsmen well."

Stuart headed for the set of sticks behind which Patel crouched. Long Man made his way to the other end, where Beharry stood in his white lab coat. Pierre handed a shiny red leather ball to Beharry, who inspected it and handed it back. Pierre tossed the ball to Jamie Cumberbatch, the newcomer from Philadelphia.

"I take it Jamie's our lead-off pitcher," Hankowsky said.

"Bowler," Watkins corrected. "He's real fast. At least, that's what he tells us."

Jamie handed his sweater to umpire Beharry, then consulted with Pierre on the field placement. Jamie wanted a more attacking field. He motioned several fielders to move in closer around Stuart.

"Come in, come in," Jamie said to Surajit.

The boy moved to within ten feet of the batsman.

"Brave little Indian boy," Stuart said.

"Don't let him frighten you," Jamie told young Bhattacharya, and motioned him to move in closer yet.

"It's your funeral," Stuart said to Surajit.

Satisfied, Jamie began walking back, polishing the ball on his shirt.

"I've gotten the hang of it so far," Hankowsky said. "The bowler's objective is to hit those sticks with the ball. So, where's he going?"

Watkins said, "In baseball terms, think of the end of the carpet as the pitcher's mound. Instead of pitching from the mound, the pitcher runs up to it and unleashes the ball, over-arm, windmill fashion. The run-up and the windmill motion enable the pitcher to hurl it with greater speed."

"Got ya."

Stuart did a perfunctory stretch, then a wiggle, wiggle, wiggle, followed by a hop, hop, hop as he loosened up. He propped the bat up against his legs, tugged on his gloves, slowly looked around the field at each fielder, and began tapping the carpet with the bat.

"This may be a stupid question," said Hankowsky.

"Go ahead anyway," Watkins invited.

"How come the umpire stands at that end, near the bowler, instead of behind the wicketkeeper at this end?"

"Part of the umpire's job, my friend, is to make sure the bowler is following a host of rules when unleashing the ball," Watkins said. "For instance, if his back foot crosses the bowler's mark before he unleashes the ball, the empire shouts 'No Ball!' It's like an error. The batsman can try to score runs off a 'No Ball' but cannot get out off such a ball. The umpire can better monitor the situation standing at that end of the carpet."

Stuart straightened himself, and, without looking back, complained to the umpire that he couldn't concentrate with all the yakking back there by "old man Watkins" and "the white guy."

"Shut your traps back there," Beharry responded.

Stuart again crouched over the bat.

"Ready?" Beharry asked Stuart.

"Ready," Stuart said.

"Coming through," the umpire said, waving Jamie to begin his run. "Right arm over."

Jamie pushed off.

"Hold it!" Beharry said, holding up his hand like a traffic cop to Jamie.

"What!" Jamie demanded.

Beharry pointed to a man in a Fernwood Bulldogs sweatshirt who had walked onto the field.

Watkins stepped toward the intruder. "There's a game going on here," he said.

The man said he was the groundsman for the Fernwood Bulldogs Little League team. He had come to prepare the field for a 4 o'clock Little League game.

"We have permission to use the field," Watkins told the baseball groundsman.

"Did you check with Max Kruger?"

"I deal with Joe Sarubbi, the recreation director," Watkins said.

"Max ain't gonna like this," the stranger said.

Hankowsky said, "Who gives a damn what Max likes!"

"Calm down," Pierre rebuked Hankowsky.

"Don't say I didn't warn you people," the stranger said, and headed back off the field.

Jamie resumed his run. His arm went up and around. The ball bounced about four feet from the batsman. Stuart waited for it to rise and swung hard. Watkins heard a sharp, cracking sound, saw Surajit turn his head and stagger, both hands going up to clutch the sides of his head. His knees buckled and he keeled over.

"Ice!" Watkins yelled, running toward the downed fielder.

"Ice!" Pierre repeated. "Somebody, bring ice!"

Fernwood players descended on Surajit, who now lay flat on his back.

"Is he dead?" asked a hovering Moses.

Patel took off his bulky wicketkeeper's gloves and used them as a cushion for the boy's head. Watkins pried Surajit's hands from his head and observed a bright red spot on the forehead. Surajit looked up with dazed eyes as a Jamaica Rebels spectator – the designated Gunga Din – arrived with a bucket of ice. Asquith created an ice pack with his handkerchief and placed it against the red spot. Surajit's massive eyelashes kept blinking and the daze seemed to lessen with each blink. Finally, he sat up on his own, probing with his fingers a lump that had appeared on the forehead.

"How do you feel?" Watkins asked.

"Goofy," Surajit said.

Watkins helped the young fielder up on his feet, stood back and watched him walk around. The boy shook his head from side to side, and assured everyone he was all right.

"Maybe you ought to sit out a bit," Pierre suggested.

Watkins handed Surajit the keys to the wagon and advised him to lie down in it. Surajit walked off, holding the ice pack to his head.

Stuart stood propped up on his bat, arms folded, looking on indifferently. "I did warn you," he said. "I also suggested you bring extra small stretchers."

"We need a sub for Surajit," Pierre said.

Cindy Asquith offered to assign her scoring duties to one of her daughters and to join Fernwood in the field. Pierre was willing to let her, but Stuart torpedoed the idea with an emphatic: "I ain't playing against no woman."

"We'll just have to play with one short," Pierre said.

Watkins sighed as he returned to third man. One delivery and one downed player. It didn't look good.

Pierre polished the ball on both legs, creating deep red smudges on his trousers before returning it to Jamie.

"He's trying to keep the shine in," Watkins said, noting Hankowsky's perplexed look. "A new, shiny ball has a lot more movement and kick to it."

Jamie's next delivery landed on the same spot on the carpet and curled to the right. Stuart swung and missed. Patel collected cleanly behind the sticks.

"That's not a strike, right?" Hankowsky said.

"No such thing in cricket," Watkins said. "You remember well."

Patel threw the ball to Watkins. He shined it some before tossing it to Hankowsky. His neighbor shined it, seemed pleased at the red smudge it created on his pants leg, and tossed it back to Jamie via Pierre.

As the next delivery came his way, Stuart stepped several paces down the carpet and waited, on tiptoes, bat upraised. He swung mightily, connected in the meat of the bat and watched as the ball sailed into the clouds. Eventually, it came down in the bushes at the back of the animated Jamaica Rebels spectators.

"Six!" shouted the bald-headed, white-bearded man.

Beharry signaled six runs to the scorers by thrusting both hands into the air.

"A home run counts as six runs," said Hankowsky. "Just checking."

"You got it," said Watkins. "And a hit along the ground past the flag is four. The batsmen don't have to run back and forth with their bats. It's automatic, and they keep on batting until they get out."

Stuart began flicking imaginary specks of dirt off the carpet with his bat as Jamie and Pierre joined a number of spectators in a search for the ball.

Watkins sat on the grass at his position. "The same ball is used throughout the inning," he told his neighbor. "We'll have to wait until they find it. Make yourself comfortable."

"How long you say this game lasts?"

"Six hours," Watkins said.

"No wonder," Hankowsky grumbled. "Can't we speed it up by using another ball?"

"That's the problem with you Americans," Watkins chided him. "Always wanting to speed things up. Relax. We'll soon have a break for water, followed by tea."

The searchers came out of the bushes with the ball, and the game resumed. The next delivery was identical, with an identical result.

"Another six!" shouted the bald-headed, white-bearded spectator, and Beharry removed any doubt about it by thrusting his hands skyward, and the search team returned to the bushes.

"You're dropping the ball too short," Patel shouted to Jamie after the search ended. "Pitch it up to the batsman."

Jamie polished the ball some more on the left leg, leaving a red smudge to match that on the right. He shortened his run-up for the fifth delivery, and reduced his pace. He obviously intended the delivery to drop closer to the batsman, following Patel's advice to "pitch it up," but Stuart apparently anticipated it. He nimbly stepped forward and whacked the ball before it could drop on the carpet.

"Six more!" the bald-headed, white-beared one roared.

The Jamaica Rebels spectators were on their feet, cheering.

"Four more!"

Now they were hollering and hooting.

Pierre took over the bowling chores. He was about to begin his first delivery when Beharry motioned him to stop and pointed to Cindy Asquith. The Englishman's wife was trotting toward the wicket from the scorers' table, scorebook in hand.

"What is it, love?" Asquith called out.

"I want a word with you, Skip," Cindy said to Pierre. "Aren't you going to let my husband bowl?"

"The game is still young," Pierre said.

"Lady," Beharry said, "please get off the field."

Jamie and Pierre operated in tandem until the ball had lost its shine and its kick.

"Try the Black Chinaman," the shrink said to Pierre.

Pierre took Sankar's advice and introduced Chong into the attack. The Black Chinaman was a spin bowler, but speed or spin, it didn't matter.

"Eighty up!" shouted Father Christmas from the Jamaica Rebels' bleachers.

Stuart drew Beharry's attention to a woman walking her dog across the lower end of the field.

"There's a game going on here, lady," Beharry scolded the woman.

"There aren't any fielders back there," she replied.

"The playing area is all the way back there," Beharry said, pointing to the flags. "You wouldn't walk across a soccer field during a game, so why are you walking across a cricket field?"

"And why are you making such a federal case out of it?" she said.

"There's a sign back there, lady: No walking the dog," Pierre said to her.

"Sue me!" she said, but she increased her pace a little just the same.

With eighty runs to their score, and no outs, Stuart decided to have a little fun. First, he slapped a delivery from Chong past Pops. As he watched Pops chase the ball in his hop-along manner, Watkins thought *There, but for the grace of God, go I.*

The ball rolled past the flag before Pops could get to it. Chong accused Pops of arbitrarily moving from deep mid-wicket to deep square leg. Pops was too pooped to protest; he simply moved to deep square leg. The next ball was hit with the same force toward mid-wicket. Pops hopped gallantly after it from deep square leg. Stuart snickered as he watched the ball beat Pops to the flags.

"Four more!"

Pierre moved Pops to the opposite side of the wicket to backward point, trying to find a safe spot for him. Then, he was shifted to deep fine leg, then back to backward point. The batsmen, firmly in control, kept finding Pops, hitting the ball a few feet to his right and to his left and over his head, making him run vainly after each hit.

Watkins felt for Pops. It wasn't that long ago when Harold Richardson Minster would have pounced cat-like on those balls, and whipped them into the wicketkeeper's glove in a flash, forcing the batsmen to dive head-first to get back. But now, he was mere entertainment for these modern-day gladiators who taunted the subject with a different type of weapon, and for the spectators who laughed and hooted as Pops chased after the ball, getting closer and closer to it but never stopping it in time. Pops' stride grew slower and slower, and his throw back of the ball weaker and weaker, and Watkins grew concerned for him.

"The man is sixty-four years old," he told Stuart. "Have a heart, will you?"

He intended no disrespect to Pops. He knew the hurt of being called old man, but if he looked like Pops did chasing those balls then they had every right to force him out of the regular lineup.

Pierre reintroduced Jamie into the attack.

Watkins heard the bat make contact with Jamie's first delivery, heard a whistling sound perilously close to his left ear, and deduced that the ball had whizzed past before he could pick it up in flight. The ball landed midway between him and the flags. He started after it. After a few paces, he reduced his stride to a stroll, trying to conserve energy, and watched the ball roll past the flags.

"I want a hundred percent from everybody," Jamie said, after Watkins had returned the ball to him.

"And I'm giving you, what, ten percent?" Watkins said.

"Okay, okay," Patel said, trying to head off a row.

The next ball, also well hit, came straight at him. Watkins ducked. It whistled past his right ear, and was past the flags when he looked back to see where it had gone. He didn't bother to chase it, but instantly glared at Jamie, braced for his reaction. Jamie glared back, hands on his hips, then asked him to switch positions with the shrink.

"You would have needed a stepladder to get that," Sankar said.

"He thinks I'm Superman, that I've got wings," Watkins said.

Their voices must have carried, for Jamie said, "At least make an effort."

And all this time, Stuart and batting partner Long Man were laughing, he-he-he-he-he, at opposite ends of the wicket.

Flustered, Watkins told himself that any more public rebuke and show of disrespect from this newcomer and he was walking off. And, unlike Beharry, he wasn't coming back. Gina was right. He was too old for this and had better things to do with his weekends.

Suddenly, a chance for an out. A delivery from Jamie caught the top edge of Stuart's bat, popped high into the air and seemed to hang forever, as if caught in some invisible netting.

"Mine," Watkins said.

"Leave it!" Jamie screamed, racing toward him.

Watkins settled beneath the ball for what he thought was an easy catch. But Jamie kept coming, hissing like a runaway locomotive. Five other guys were closer but Jamie must have considered himself their newly discovered savior, and he wanted to take the credit for that catch.

"Mine," Watkins repeated, more assertively.

"Just one person," Pierre called out. Not wanting to pick sides, he left it up to Jamie and Watkins to work it out.

"Back off," Watkins said, for Jamie was still what seemed a long way off.

"Leave it!" Jamie yelled, and it was an order this time. "Leave it! Leave it! Leave it!"

"I've got it!" Watkins had it, felt the crash, and didn't have it anymore.

"Jesus Christ!" Jamie screamed. They lay on their stomachs facing each other. "I told you to leave it."

"I had it," Watkins said, picking up the ball.

"Somebody, throw the friggin' ball!" Patel cried.

Stuart and batting partner Long Man scampered for one run, crossed again, and turned for a third.

Jamie, snarling, grabbed the ball away from Watkins and hurled it toward the wicketkeeper as the batsmen safely completed the third. The throw was wide of Patel and, with no one backing up, the ball raced to the opposite boundary for four extras.

Seven runs had been scored off that one delivery. Watkins didn't think it could get any worse.

At that point, Beharry, mercifully, called for a ten-minute water break.

2:35 p.m.

Watkins checked the scorebook, saw Hankowsky beneath a shade tree reading *The Rules of Cricket*, and reported the score to him: 149 runs with no outs. Hankowsky already had read the part that said ten outs comprised an inning.

"Looks like we'll be here the entire weekend trying to get them out," he said.

"Relax," Watkins said. "This is bush-league cricket. Under the improvised rules, their inning ends at 4 o'clock, regardless of the number of outs. Then we try to top their score."

Watkins went to his wagon. He found Surajit leaning against the vehicle, massaging his forehead. The lump was barely discernible, but Surajit balked at the prospect of returning to the field.

Watkins called home on his cell phone. No answer. What did it mean?

A beat-up convertible Thunderbird with the top down rolled to a stop near the wagon. A muscular man in skin-tight white clothes got out. He wore earrings. A chain, with a bat-shaped pendant, hung halfway down his chest. Their eyes met.

"You're not Emile Pierre, are you?" the man asked, and Watkins detected a Jamaican accent.

Watkins pointed out Pierre. The man thanked him and headed that way. Watkins dialed again. Still, no answer. He decided he would try again later.

About forty spectators had joined Fernwood's camp. The visitors included a cute blond, early twenties, in a spaghetti-strapped tank top, bare midriff with a rose tattoo below her belly button, Levi's and black leather boots. Jamie was showing the blond a cricket ball and telling her about it - how it was a little smaller than a baseball and much harder, with a cork interior and leather exterior with one seam.

Watkins spotted Pops on the grass, his back propped against the end of the bleachers. He was breathing hard and there was white spittle at the corners of his mouth. Watkins took a bottle of water from Pierre's bag over to him.

"Take your time," Watkins said, tilting, and Pops gulped.

Watkins felt a tap on his shoulder. It was Pierre, with the newcomer. "Watkins, this is Napoleon," Pierre said. "You've heard of him."

He sure had. Napoleon Bonaparte was part of a growing legion of cricketers who either once played for the prestigious West Indies national team or came close to making the team. With no useful skill outside of cricket, they now eked out a livelihood shuttling from cricket league to cricket league in the United States and Canada, selling their services to the highest bidders.

"Excuse us a second," Pierre said to Napoleon, and drew Watkins aside. "He arrived in Philadelphia this morning from Toronto looking for work. He called up International and they told him we were looking for players. He wants two hundred dollars. I figure he can sub for Surajit."

As the one in charge of the club's purse strings, Watkins took pride in the fact that all collected dues were used for the intended purposes. Paying washed-up players wasn't one of them. "I'd rather play short," he told Pierre.

"Hey, Jamaica Rebels have 149 runs on the board," Pierre said. "At the rate they're going, they're likely to score 400, then bowl us out for less than 50. Napoleon's the fastest bowler around. He can stop them dead in their tracks. He's also handy with the bat."

Watkins studied Napoleon. The athlete raised his head and stared at him with squinting eyes. Watkins felt a tremor. The man was, indeed, intimidating.

"Just this once," Watkins decided.

Napoleon took checks.

"Let's see if it's okay with the umpire," Pierre said.

They took Napoleon over to umpire Beharry, who was feeding his face with peas and rice from a bowl, scooping up the meal with his fingers. Pierre asked Beharry's permission for Napoleon to sub for Surajit.

"Sorry," Beharry said. "The game's too far gone to switch players. However, if the Jamaica Rebels captain doesn't object, fine with me."

They approached Stuart, standing in the shade squirting Perrier into his mouth. "Well, if it ain't ole Nappy putting in another cameo," Stuart greeted Napoleon. "How much are they paying you?"

"The umpire says it's too late to get me in the game," Napoleon answered. "He's afraid I might hurt you with my fastball."

Stuart took the bait. "Let him play," he told Beharry. "His bowling is mediocre and he doesn't know which end of the bat is up."

As Pierre was instructing the scorers to make the lineup change, a commotion erupted among the spectators. The source turned out to be a bulldog at the end of a leash. A man in a purple turban and a gas-station navy blue outfit was at the other end of the leash, trying to restrain the animal, which was trying to get a piece of everyone in its path.

Watkins recognized the new stranger. "I see you made it," he said to Bhupinder Singh, and drew back when the animal made a rush at him.

"I called up my cousin to work the gas station for me," Singh said.

Watkins reminded Pierre of Singh's claim that he had played against Imran Khan during a Pakistan visit to the Indian state of Punjab.

Pierre shrugged. "Imran Khan would have played against hundreds of cricketers, good, bad and mediocre, during his career. Besides, we've already got an eleven."

Watkins thought that now would have been an opportune time to drop out of the game to make way for Singh. But if Gina had decided to play hardball and rearrange their schedule for the evening, then no sense in his rushing home. He could deal with it later. Instead of stepping down, he pointed to Pops, seated now on a lawn chair, the flask of the white rum to his lips.

As he approached him, Watkins saw Pops slip the flask into its hiding place beneath the bleachers and light a cigarette with the butt of another cigarette.

"How do you feel?" Watkins asked.

"Fine," Pops said.

"We have a new guy just arrived. He played with Imran Khan...."

"I ain't stepping down," Pops interrupted, and refused to budge.

Watkins explained the situation to Singh and the Sikh said, "I really came to see your lawyer."

"I handle negligence cases," Pierre said to Singh. "Slip 'n falls. Nothing heavy. According to what Watkins told me, sounds as though you need a criminal lawyer."

"Maybe we talk anyway, after the game," Singh said.

Beharry returned to the middle, signaling the end of the water break.

Pierre called the troops together for another pep talk. "Okay, guys," he said, all juiced up. "We've got one of the best bowlers in America here in Napoleon. Let's give him a hundred and twenty percent."

The players upped the ante, agreeing to give him two hundred percent.

"Don't forget my husband," Cindy Asquith said to Pierre as Fernwood players returned to the field with a new bounce to their steps. "He's really a good bowler."

Her daughters joined in the entreaty. Pierre merely smiled, and handed the ball to Napoleon.

"You might want to send for your helmet," Napoleon said to Stuart.

"Boy, you're really scaring me now." Stuart began shivering wildly as if struck by electricity. "Can't stop shaking."

Napoleon set his field in consultation with Pierre. Then Pierre was counting heads. "Somebody's missing," the captain said.

Watkins did his own count, three times. There were ten players on the field.

"It's Pretty Boy," said Patel.

"Who's Pretty Boy?" Watkins asked.

"The new player," said Patel. "Jamie Cumberbatch."

Cindy reported that Jamie was last seen strolling toward the parking lot with the blond girl. She believed she saw him drive off with her in a Porsche. Pierre didn't think that was possible, considering that "Pretty Boy" had hitched a ride to the grounds. Cindy surmised that it must have been Blondie's Porsche.

Pierre raised the possibility of bringing in Singh for Jamie. Beharry asked Stuart whether he minded.

"Don't make a bit of difference to me," Stuart said.

Singh was given the good news. The Sikh tied the dog to the back of the bleachers. He was about to join the fielders when a new problem arose: Beharry pointed to Singh's "gas station clothes" and explained that it was in violation of the league's dress code.

"Let the man play," Stuart said.

Beharry granted an exemption.

Napoleon took a fifty-yard run up and unleashed a zinger. Stuart swung, missed completely and was struck on the left pad.

Napoleon jumped into the air with upraised hands. "Howszat!"

Beharry stood rigid, hands in his pockets.

"Oh, Gawd, de man out!" Napoleon screamed at Beharry.

"He ain't out till I say he's out," Beharry said.

"What game are you watching, man?" Napoleon yelled.

"No talking back," Beharry said. "Otherwise, I put you off the field."

Patel retrieved and threw the ball back to Napoleon, who slammed it into the carpet, then kicked it viciously. Beharry took a pen and notebook out of his lab coat and duly recorded the unsportsmanlike conduct.

"What happened there?" Hankowsky wanted to know.

"The batsman is supposed to stop the ball with his bat, not his leg," Watkins explained. "Stuart got hit on the leg pad and Napoleon appealed for LBW."

"Leg Before Wicket?" Hankowsky said, with some pride.

"Right," Watkins said. "In this case, the wicket refers to the sticks. In Napoleon's opinion, the ball would have struck the sticks, or wicket, had Stuart's leg not got in the way."

Stuart again complained to the umpire about "the yakking back there," and Beharry again warned the players not to disturb the batsman's concentration.

Napoleon threw down another bullet of a delivery that again rapped Stuart on the padded leg.

Hankowsky did an imitation of Napoleon, jumping in the air with upraised hands. "Howszat!" He looked around, realized he was the only one who had appealed, and said to Beharry, "Never mind."

Stuart struck Napoleon's third delivery hard back to the bowler. Conventional wisdom said Napoleon should have jumped out of the way. Instead, he went down, caught the ball cleanly inches from the ground with both hands, rolled over twice and rose triumphantly, throwing the ball into the air.

Watkins joined in the rush to offer Napoleon high-fives for the brilliant catch. Stuart hadn't moved.

"What's going on here?" Napoleon demanded of Beharry.

"No ball!" Beharry said.

"What!" Napoleon screamed, and ran toward the umpire with murderous intent.

Pierre intercepted Napoleon, and Watkins joined in restraining him.

"His back foot crossed the line," Beharry said, and he demonstrated what he claimed Napoleon did, first planting his entire right boot on the bowler's mark, then lifting the back part of the boot to show that Napoleon's foot was an inch or so over the line when he unleashed the ball.

Pierre said, "If it's a 'no ball' you're supposed to make the call before the batsman offers a stroke, not after."

"I made the call early," Beharry said.

"You never made the call!" Napoleon accused Beharry.

"I heard it," Stuart said from the other end of the carpet. "He shouted 'no ball!' loud and clear."

Napoleon turned to Stuart. "You know you're out! Do the honorable thing and walk."

"Don't beg," Stuart said.

"Told you the umpire's a bloody cheat," said Asquith. "He came here as their twelfth man." He turned to Watkins. "Never pay an umpire first. All his big speech about playing fair. He didn't fool me."

"What do you expect?" said Chong. "He's from Guyana."

"That wasn't necessary," Sankar, the shrink, chided the Black Chinaman.

"I have a good mind to punch your face," Napoleonsaid to Beharry.

"Oh, yeah?" Beharry uprooted one of the three sticks at his end of the carpet. "Come on," he said, stepping back. "Come punch my face."

"I don't believe this," Watkins said to Beharry. "You can't be serious."

"I serious," said Beharry, and waved the stick back and forth like a magic wand. "He really get me vex now!"

"I see you settle disputes the old-fashioned way," Hankowsky said to Watkins, who braced himself to intervene again.

"Come on!" Beharry continued to challenge Napoleon. "Punch away."

"You want to fight me?" Napoleon said, pointing to his own chest. "A little cross-eyed man like you wants to fight me?"

"He didn't mean it," Watkins begged off for Beharry, seeking to pacify the advancing Napoleon. "Who ever heard of an umpire fighting?"

"You're right." Beharry threw the stick away. "I can't allow myself to stoop to his level." Beharry took off his lab coat, folded and laid it over his left arm, and began walking toward the Jamaica Rebels' camp.

"See that?" the Englishman said to Watkins. "Told you, you shouldn't have paid him in advance."

"You've made your point," Watkins said.

"Okay, okay," Pierre called out to Beharry. "You said you called 'No Ball.' We give you the benefit of the doubt. Gentlemen, let's all settle down and play decent cricket."

Beharry continued walking.

"Don't worry about him," Stuart said. "He's just grandstanding."

"But he already got paid," Asquith said. "He doesn't have to finish the game."

"He may have gotten paid but he doesn't have a ride home," Stuart said, raising his voice loud enough for the umpire to hear.

Beharry did a U-turn. "Look, I call it the way I see it, okay? I don't play favorites."

"Did they pay you off?" Napoleon asked Beharry.

"We all know they did," said Pierre. "Let's get on with it anyway."

Napoleon wanted a more aggressive field. Pierre obliged by bringing in his fielders closer around the batsman. Napoleon was about to begin his run up when Stuart signaled to his teammates off field to bring him "fresh lumber." Two of Stuart's teammates arrived, each with a half-dozen bats. Stuart tested each one, tap, tap, tapping it on the carpet.

Pierre accused Stuart of holding up the game. A still agitated Beharry replied that he was the one who decided who held up the game or not.

Stuart eventually selected a bigger bat with a longer handle. "Okay," he said, waving it at Napoleon, "bowl your shit to me."

Napoleon walked way back to the flags and ran up. His right arm became a blur. Watkins never saw the ball leave his hand, or in flight. He heard a loud rattling sound after the arm came down, and saw the three sticks behind Stuart take flight.

"Bowled!" Napoleon screamed, dropping to both knees, leaning back and shaking clenched fists at the sky.

Stuart didn't wait for Beharry's decision. He tucked the bat beneath his arm and began peeling his gloves off as he strode off the field.

"Hey, you!" Napoleon called after Stuart, even as he accepted his teammates' high-fives and back slaps. "Where are you going? The umpire ain't put you out, so where are you going? He! He! He! He!"

Watkins joined in the laughter.

"One down, nine to go," Hankowsky said to himself.

"Try the Sikh," Asquith said to Pierre. "Let's see what he can do."

Pierre took the advice and threw the ball to Bhupinder Singh. The Sikh rearranged the field. Unlike Napoleon, he wanted a defensive field. Everyone was to drop back.

"Gully," he said to Watkins, and motioned him to where gully was.

Watkins appreciated that.

Singh loosened up by bowling a few trial balls to Pierre. When he was ready, he did a one-two-three step run up, and tossed a slow, high, arching delivery to Zig-Zag, the new batsman.

"Oh, no!" Watkins groaned at the poor delivery.

Zig-Zag waited with upraised bat for the ball to get to him on the full, and swung hard.

Crack!

Watkins groaned louder as he watched the ball kiss the skies. It was coming down a good three feet over Moses' head near a flag when the youngster reached into his back pocket, whipped out his baseball mitt, leaped, and snatched it out of the air.

"How's that, umpire?" Singh asked Beharry, almost politely.

"Don't be ridiculous," Beharry replied.

"This ain't baseball," Zig-Zag added.

Pierre stepped in. "Show me in the rule book where it says you can't use a baseball glove to catch a cricket ball."

Beharry consulted *The Laws of Cricket*. He flipped, and kept on flipping back and forth. Pierre had raised an interesting point and his teammates crowded around Beharry for an answer. Beharry gave up and raised a finger.

"You can't do that!" Zig-Zag advanced on Beharry with upraised bat.

Beharry put his finger down.

"You already put the man out," Pierre said to Beharry. "You can't change your mind."

Beharry put his finger back up.

Zig-Zag got into a shouting match with the umpire about his flip-flopping.

From off field, Stuart shouted for his man to come out, that he shouldn't worry about being cheated out because Jamaica Rebels had "plenty of batting left." Zig-Zag tossed aside his bat en route to the Jamaica Rebels' camp. His gloves were next, then his pads, and his protective box.

Watkins gave Moses a congratulatory high-five. "Nice catch," he told the boy.

Pierre offered to sign him up permanently. "We need young blood," he said to Watkins, as a grinning Moses swaggered back to his fielding position.

"Two outs, eight to go," said Hankowsky.

The incoming batsman went for a big hit off a similar floater from Singh, missed, and the ball knocked the middle stick down.

"Next!" Napoleon yelled at the Jamaica Rebels' camp.

Three outs with no addition to the score. Watkins was elated.

The next man up hit the first ball he received from Singh to Hankowsky's right and started to run. Hankowsky darted after the ball, gathered and whipped it into Patel's wicketkeeper's gloves. Patel knocked the sticks down with the ball before Batsman No. 5 could scamper back.

Watkins joined in the appeal. Beharry's finger went up.

"I ain't out," the batsman protested.

"Get the hell outta here!" Napoleon said, waving him off.

Hankowsky accepted the all-round congratulations for the sharp throw in to Patel, but he wanted to know why Patel didn't throw to the other end for a double play.

"No such thing in cricket, my friend," said a jubilant Watkins.

"Right," said Hankowsky.

Eight runs later, Napoleon uprooted all three sticks with a rocket of a delivery, and went on to achieve a hat-trick - with Patel taking a diving catch for the second out and Moses hauling down another high one just inside the boundary with his gloves for the third.

Seven outs with the addition of only eight runs since the water break. Watkins was ecstatic.

Pops grabbed at a ball that was batted straight to his chest off Singh's bowling. It pelted him back a foot or two, and knocked him over, but he held on to the ball. Watkins pulled him up, and Pops kept on grinning and grinning at his feat.

Then, it was Watkins' turn. The ball was slapped to his right. Not wanting to be accused of giving less than the agreed two hundred percent, Watkins flung his left hand, open-palmed, in the general direction of the ball. He felt a stinging sensation, pulled the hand back, examined his palm and, to his surprise, found himself looking at the little red ball.

Watkins heard his teammates roar, saw them running-toward him, and casually tossed the ball over his shoulder as the pros tended to do after making a difficult catch look easy. The shrink lifted him from behind and the others took turns rubbing his head and slapping his back.

"That," said Pierre "was vintage Watkins."

Even Napoleon was impressed. "You must have been quite a cricketer in your day," he said.

Just wait till you see me bat, Watkins thought.

Nine outs, one to go.

The last batsman was a Stuart clone. He stretched, wiggled, tapped his bat and hopped about before settling down.

"Ready?" Beharry asked him.

"Ready," the batsman said.

Singh threw up yet another floater. The ball dropped wide of the sticks and out of the batsman's reach. It must have struck a pebble or a rough spot on the carpet, for it veered sharply and hit the sticks. The batsman hadn't offered a stroke.

"I wasn't ready," he complained to Beharry.

"Too bad," Watkins said, and trotted with his teammates off the field.

"That's it," Hankowsky said, alongside. "Ten outs. The eleventh batsman doesn't have a partner, so the inning is over. He'll be listed in the scorebook as 'not out.'"

"You are a fast learner," Watkins said.

Timmy stepped onto the field with the TV camera on his shoulder. Hankowsky beamed and gave thumbs up. "Did you get me with that absolutely brilliant piece of fielding?" he asked his son.

"Yep," Timmy said.

"Told you, the old man still has it."

Jamaica Rebels had crashed from 149 runs with no outs at the break to 162 all out within minutes of the resumption.

Everyone was crowing.

Except Cindy. "How come you didn't let my husband bowl?" she asked Pierre.

"We didn't need his bowling today," Pierre said, and Watkins smiled at the familiar line. "But we'll be relying on his batting."

That wasn't good enough for the Englishman's wife. "What's the matter? You don't want him to win MVP?"

Watkins checked with Stuart about what type of food his players wanted. The Jamaica Rebels captain said they preferred to eat after the game rather than between innings and they weren't fussy about the type of food. In the meantime, they were indulging themselves with bake and codfish, ginger beer and an assortment of Jamaican delights handed out by their followers. They also patronized their own traveling snow cone and fry-fish vendors.

One of the vendors carried six-ounce bottles labeled "Love Potions" that he touted as the best aphrodisiac on the market. Watkins saw Hankowsky examining one of the six-ounce bottles. The label featured a drawing of a naked couple intertwined in bed.

"What does a virile man like you want with that stuff?" he asked his neighbor.

"He says it enhances performance," Hankowsky said.

"It does," the vendor said. "Specially grown herbs, imported from the islands. Better than Viagra."

"Is it approved by the Food and Drug Administration?" Hankowsky asked the vendor.

"FDA approved!" the vendor sneered. "Shit! If they approve this stuff the big drug companies would be out of business. The government won't let no black immigrant do that!"

"Yeah, but is it safe?" Hankowsky said.

"Never had a complaint," the vendor said.

Hankowsky picked up another bottle.

"That's the Number Ten," the vendor said. "Powerful stuff. You don't want that, unless you have erectile dysfunction. It's guaranteed to get your thing up, but not down. Could be embarrassing, if you know what I mean."

Hankowsky forked over forty dollars for two bottles of the Number Nine. The vendor threw in a small, unlabeled package of dried leaves that he said also helped the sex drive and he advised Hankowsky how to brew it to maximum strength and the temperature at which it should be sipped to enjoy the rich flavor.

Watkins shook his head at his friend and returned to his wagon. Surajit was sleeping in the backseat. Watkins called the neighborhood pizzeria and ordered six large pies, soda, and supplies. He then called home.

"Dad, where are you?" Maggie answered.

His daughter's voice rattled him.

"Dad?"

It occurred to him that Maggie would have recognized his cell phone number on caller ID. "Where's your mother?"

"Mom's here. So are Stephen and Edward. The question is: Where are you?"

"Tell your mother I've taken care of the problem," he said. "She can go ahead and prepare the chicken for the grill. I'll be home in a few minutes to fire it up."

"It's too late for that; she's already started dinner."

Gina had to have given up on him. Or maybe she was just trying to make a point. "Then tell her don't worry about dessert," he said. "I'll pick up something on the way home."

Maggie sighed. "Okay, Dad."

Asquith had brought an ample supply of cucumber sandwiches to hold them until the main course arrived. The sandwiches went well with what was left of Pops' beef patties.

Pierre sat at the scorers' table mulling over the team's batting order.

Watkins kneeled beside him. "Skip, can I ask a favor?"

"I forgot: You've got to go," Pierre said. "No problem."

Watkins should have been happy. Not only had he organized the game and gotten Patel to accept responsibility for the rest of the season, but had contributed with what everyone agreed was a magnificent catch. Vintage Watkins, as Pierre had said. For what better last hurrah could he ask? And now he was free to leave to repair any damage with Gina, permission of the captain. But the adrenaline still flowed and he wanted to get in a few good whacks.

"How about if I open the inning?" he asked Pierre.

"Nah," Pierre said. "We really don't need you."

Watkins took it as an insult. "You don't think I can play their pace bowling?"

"You're taking it the wrong way," Pierre said. "They've made a relatively low score, and we've got Napoleon, and we've got Singh. If what he says about having played with Imran Khan is true, Singh should really give us a lift."

Watkins didn't push it. To do so would be to beg and it was beneath him to beg. He could leave, dignity intact.

Pierre called Hankowsky over, and asked him whether he wanted to open the inning.

"Why not?" Hankowsky said.

Watkins squirmed. In the real world, a novice like Hankowsky would have been placed at the bottom of the batting order, when the bowlers would have lost their fire and the ball its shine and kick. Pierre no doubt was gambling that Hankowsky would hit the ball with the same power he had demonstrated during his warm-up with his son Timmy and the kid Moses.

Watkins was concerned for Hankowsky. The TV cameraman may have been a fast learner, but he seemed oblivious to the fact that being sent in to face the Jamaica Rebels' front-line bowlers was akin to infantrymen crossing mine fields in advance of the main invading force: mere fodder for the cannons.

Watkins accompanied Hankowsky to his TV-8 van, assisted him in padding up and watched him walk around, robot-like, weighed down with leg, arm, thigh and shoulder pads, gloves, and helmet.

"Let's see you run," Watkins said.

Hankowsky ran a few yards. The heavy foot pads kept rubbing against each other and he almost tripped. Watkins adjusted the straps and told him to try again. Hankowsky did better the second time.

Vijay Patel was his opening partner.

The Jamaica Rebels took to the field, accompanied by Beharry in his white lab coat.

"Send in the clowns," Stuart called out from midfield.

"Show some respect," Pierre shouted back.

Hankowsky and Patel waited for Timmy to grab the camera before striding out.

"Take your time," Pierre said to their backs. "We've got the whole day."

Watkins found himself caught up in the excitement and decided to watch a few minutes of his team's inning.

The opening batsmen were nearing the carpet when a voice cut through the all-round applause: "Vijay!"

The sound came from the parking lot. Watkins looked over and saw a woman in a sari on the edge of the grass.

"Vijay!" she yelled.

Padded up the way Patel was, with his red helmet on, Watkins thought it would have been impossible for Mrs. Patel to recognize her husband. It must have been his gait, the way his body rocked, like a hiker going uphill, that gave Patel away.

Patel must not have heard his wife because he kept walking alongside Hankowsky.

"Vijay, your wife's calling you," crowed the bald-headed, white-bearded man.

"Vijay!" Mrs. Patel said.

Patel turned toward his wife, started to run the other way, then, apparently realizing he had been caught red-handed, took a bold stand: He resumed walking toward the carpet.

"Vijay!" Mrs. Patel screamed. "I'm your wife!"

Patel stopped. "This," he said to her, holding up his bat and pumping as though milking a cow, "is my wife!"

Mrs. Patel brought both hands up to her mouth. She stood there, seemingly struck dumb, then turned and ran back to the parking lot amid raucous hooting from the Jamaica Rebels' camp.

Watkins felt her pain, and was concerned about what it meant for him. Would Patel be able to fulfill his duties as manager? If not, who would take over?

Stuart handed the ball to Zig-Zag.

"Knock their brains out," shouted grandfather.

It was immediately apparent how Zig-Zag came by that name. He had an unorthodox run-up to the bowler's mark, zigging this way and zagging that way, playing peek a-boo behind Beharry before releasing the ball.

Zig-Zag hammered the first delivery mid-carpet. The ball rose and crashed into Patel's helmet before he could take evasive action. The batsman collapsed. Watkins looked out anxiously with his teammates for signs that Patel might be hurt. After long seconds, Patel rose from the carpet, and craned his neck, making sure his head was still intact.

Zig-Zag's second delivery was identical. Patel again ducked, this time throwing up his arms defensively as he did so. The ball caught the top edge of the bat. It popped up but fell safely halfway to the flags. By the time the ball was fielded and returned to Zig-Zag, Patel and Hankowsky had crossed twice.

"Patel's off the mark," Pierre said for those who didn't see it or simply because it felt good saying it.

Zig-Zag's third delivery was more of the same. This time Patel elected to have a swipe, missed and was hit on the helmet. Again, he went down.

Watkins joined in the booing from Fernwood's camp. Pierre started onto the field to register a protest. Beharry ordered him off. Patel rose shakily. He took the helmet off and touched the side of his head and looked at his hand. He put the helmet back on.

Zig-Zag threw down a thunderbolt and Patel ducked cleanly this time.

Another rocket. Another duck.

Then Patel took a direct hit to the helmet.

Watkins ran onto the field, shouting "Ice! Somebody, ice!" Getting to the downed Patel, he observed that the blow had cracked the helmet and left a gash above the left temple. Blood flowed.

Shrugging off his teammates' efforts to get him to sit still, Patel rose on his own before the cubes of ice wrapped in a handkerchief arrived. He made no attempt to stop the flow of blood down the side of his face and onto his shirt.

Watkins marched up to Stuart. "Fernwood is ending the game right now!"

"Pull your men off and you lose," Stuart said.

"You can have the points." Watkins knew he was overstepping. As captain, Pierre should have been the one making such an important decision, but he was mad enough with Pierre to preempt him. "Come on, guys," he said to Patel and Hankowsky, "the game is over. They win."

Stuart said to Zig-Zag, "They can't play the bouncers and beamers. No more bouncers and beamers."

Watkins continued to lead his players off the field, carrying Patel's bat and helmet. Pierre tagged along, head bowed.

"Hold it," Beharry said, and proceeded to assure Fernwood that, as umpire, he wouldn't allow the deliberate attempt to injure the batsmen.

Pierre asserted himself, agreeing to continue, but under protest. Patel, holding the ice pack to his head, opted to continue, but Pierre didn't want to risk another injury.

Watkins put an arm around Patel's shoulder and squeezed. "He's right, my friend. Better go home. Make it up to your wife."

Patel was listed as "retired hurt" in the scorebook. Watkins hoped that Pierre would send him in next. Instead, Pierre sent in Napoleon as Batsman No. 3. Watkins tried to stifle the hurt.

The seven-foot-tall Jack Long, aka Long Man, aka String Bean, relieved Zig-Zag. Hankowsky was the facing batsman.

"Looks like we've got ourselves a rabbit here," Stuart said, and asked his fielders to crowd Hankowsky.

The TV cameraman started to tap his bat on the carpet. As Long Man began his run-up, Hankowsky switched to a baseball stance, swung, missed, and the three sticks went flying. He came out to tepid applause.

"Sorry," Hankowsky apologized. "I had that sucker right in my sights. Don't see how I could have missed."

"Next time," Watkins said.

"I got it on film," Timmy said, and Hankowsky grimaced.

Two outs, with only two runs on the board. Fernwood was off to a typical Fernwood start, Watkins thought. At this rate, perhaps he'd a chance to bat after all.

Pierre went in as Batsman No. 4.

"Just one ball for the skip," Stuart said to Long Man.

And one ball it was. It struck his right pad.

"Howszat!"

Beharry forgot himself and joined in the loud appeal to himself. He caught himself, put on a stern demeanor, and stuck his finger in the air, signaling Pierre out Leg Before Wicket, the action provoking laughter in the Jamaica Rebels' offside camp.

"That ball was way outside the sticks," Pierre fumed as he came in. "Someone ought to shoot that umpire."

Asquith, Batsman No. 5, strode out to applause from his wife and a couple of flips from his two cheerleading daughters. He went for a big hit, no doubt trying to show off, and was caught on the boundary without scoring.

"Next!" Stuart yelled to Pierre.

Chong, No. 6, went out to join Napoleon, Batsman No.3. The Black Chinaman thought he had the power to hit the ball over the flags, but got out as Asquith did, without scoring.

And just like that, half the side was down for two runs.

The Sikh, Batsman No. 7, was next.

Observing that the Sikh wasn't wearing a helmet, Watkins grabbed one from the team's kit and took it to him. "Here. Put this on."

Singh smiled, and waved him off. Brave man, Watkins thought. Or more likely he didn't wear a helmet because it wouldn't have fit over the turban. At the wicket, the Sikh stretched, jumped up and down, tap-tapped the bat.

"Let's get on with it," Stuart said to him. "I've got a wedding to go to."

The Sikh kept limbering up. Finally, he settled down. But not quite. He rose up and, like a periscope above water, scanned the horizon.

Long Man unleashed a zinger. Singh stepped forward, and swung fluidly. He didn't bother to run, nor did Watkins expect him to. It was clear from the arc and the speed of ascent that the ball was headed for the bushes.

"Six!" Fernwood's camp roared, and Beharry held both hands straight up.

The ball was returned and the promise of no more bouncers and beamers was forgotten. Long Man hammered the next delivery into the ground. Singh should have taken evasive action as the ball rose toward his head. Instead, the lefty leaned back, swung and watched as the ball sailed into the parking lot and landed on the roof of an SUV.

"Six more!"

Watkins joined in the laughter as a Jamaica Rebels spectator ran toward the lot, presumably to inspect the damage to his sports utility vehicle. Watkins observed that Patel wasn't part of the merriment. He had put on his suit and tie, and sat off to himself on a lawn chair, staring vacantly out into the field.

Watkins went to him. "Do you need a ride home?"

"She shouldn't have embarrassed me like that," he said, as if to himself.

"Yeah, but think of how she's feeling," Watkins said. "I mean, guys like Pierre, Pops and I, we've been married a long time. The first time is the worst, believe me."

Cindy joined in the entreaty, and offered to take him home and to put in a good word for him with Mrs. Patel. He accepted the offer.

"Stick your head in a whirlpool when you get home," Stuart shouted from the field at the retreating Patel.

"Better not," Zig-Zag said. "Your wife might keep it down!"

The runs came at a fast clip.

"Singh's got his fifty!" Pierre said, and the Sikh raised his bat in acknowledgement of his contribution of fifty runs.

Beharry halted play to chase off the field two bikini-clad women who had strolled onto a corner of the field to sunbathe.

The Jamaica Rebels brought on their slow bowlers, then a new pair of fast bowlers, but it didn't seem to matter; the runs continued to flow.

Napoleon and Singh were taking a fast run when the string that kept the turban in place snapped. Singh's hair broke from its confinement and spilled down his back and covered his face. Singh pocketed the cloth and kept on batting, taking on the appearance of a wild man with his hair swishing around as he ran amok, slashing, hooking and stepping out to lift the ball repeatedly outside the circle of flags into the bushes and the parking lot, where several spectators had positioned themselves in an attempt to minimize the damage to their vehicles.

Forgetting his own hurt pride, Watkins was delirious as he watched the Jamaica Rebels hotshots fall apart. One walked off the field after Zig-Zag berated him for failing to take what the bowler said was an easy catch. Another fielder dropped a real bullet off the Sikh's bat. This time, Stuart delivered the tongue-lashing. The fielder, too, stormed off, accusing Stuart of bad captaincy.

"A hundred up!" Pierre said after another massive hit by the Sikh.

The Fernwood camp, sensing an unlikely victory, was on its feet, cheering every stroke, even those that didn't produce runs.

"Singh and Napoleon got a hundred-run partnership," Pierre announced minutes later.

A few swings of the bat later, "Singh's got his century."

The Sikh again raised his bat in acknowledgment of the applause for his individual score of one hundred runs, and accepted Napoleon's congratulations by punching the general's gloved hand.

Watkins checked the score. His team needed thirty runs to tie Jamaica Rebels' score, and thirty-one to win. "It's in the bag," he said, with no room for doubt.

The loud barking of the bulldog alerted them to an intrusion within their ranks.

"Who's in charge?" the intruder demanded.

Watkins saw his teammates look his way and acknowledged that he was.

"Got to get off the field, big guy," the intruder said. "We've got a game to play."

"And just who are you?" Watkins asked, taking stock of the chunky, balding, fiftyish man in green warm-up suit with the words Fernwood Little League on the chest and the association's logo of a fern stitched across the left shoulder.

"My name," the stranger said with what sounded to Watkins like a German accent, "is Maximilian Kruger."

4:15 p.m.

Tony, the sod man, had warned him about Max Kruger. So had the groundsman for the Little League. In person, Kruger appeared every bit the bully he had been told to expect, but Watkins wasn't fazed.

"We have permission to use this field," he told Kruger. "We leave when our game is through."

Snakelike lines appeared across Kruger's forehead. "This field is assigned to the Fernwood Little League, and you're trespassing." Kruger pointed toward the parking lot. Vehicles were pulling up and adults and youngsters in baseball uniforms and bats were spilling out. "Our kids need the field to play. Now!"

"I assume you do have a permit," Pierre said to Kruger. "If so, may I see it?"

Kruger said, "I think you people better leave the field before I call the township police."

Hankowsky confronted Kruger. "You people! And who exactly is you people!"

"Calm down," Pierre said to Hankowsky. "Watkins is our liaison to the recreation director. Let Watkins handle it."

Watkins said to Kruger, "There were cleat marks across our wicket. I take it your players were responsible."

Kruger turned a darker shade of red. "This ain't Africa or India."

Watkins heard cries of indignation at his back. Even the dog started barking and straining on the leash, wanting a piece of Maximilian Kruger. The intruder stood his ground, glaring with laser eyes. Here was a man who clearly was used to having his way.

Watkins stared back. "I think you better leave."

"You don't know who you're dealing with," Kruger said, without blinking. "You're about to find out."

"The number is 9-1-1," Hankowsky said. "Do you need a cell phone?"

"Ihr seid Arschloecher!" Kruger snarled, with a backward glance.

"Up yours, too!" Hankowsky said.

"That wasn't necessary," Watkins chided the cameraman. "You have to be diplomatic."

"Diplomacy," Hankowsky said, "is a two-way street."

Watkins turned his attention back to the field. The encounter with Kruger had unnerved him. The team had had its share of scheduling conflicts over the years with a host of clubs, but they were all resolved by the athletes themselves without animosity. This one, however, appeared headed for a showdown. That meant he would have to stick around a bit longer to deal with the cops, if Kruger did call them out.

Stuart had brought Zig-Zag back into the attack.

His confidence built up by his lengthy stay at the wicket with Singh, Napoleon drove the next ball back past the bowler, and Long Man gave chase. Long Man stopped the ball a foot or so just short of the flags. Singh, halfway down the carpet, kept calling for the run, then tried to scramble back. Long Man's throw in to the bowler, hovering over the sticks at the non-striker's end, was perfect. Singh didn't wait for the umpire's decision.

The Sikh came out to a standing ovation.

Watkins patted him on the back. "Thought you said you were rusty."

"I try," Singh said, and flashed the gold in his upper.

Watkins checked with the scorers.

"We need ten runs to tie, eleven to win," Cindy reported.

Sankar was next man in. Pierre told him the score, and gave his standard advice: "Take your time."

The shrink was struck on the pad with the first ball he faced. Beharry put a finger up, although no one had appealed for LBW. Sankar, enraged, challenged the call. Beharry threatened to report him to the league's disciplinary committee for questioning the decision.

Pierre stormed onto the field. "This is wholesale robbery," he said to Stuart. "We need a new umpire. That's the only way we'll continue."

Stuart rejected the idea, but relented when Pierre threatened to forfeit the game. Stuart recommended Father Christmas as substitute umpire.

"No way," Pierre said. "We need a neutral umpire."

Finding one, however, became a problem.

"I'll umpire," Asquith said from the bleachers, hand upraised. "I play fair."

Stuart studied the Englishman. "Sure," he said. "Let the record show that Beharry ain't feeling too good, and.... What's your name?"

"Shane Asquith."

"Let the record show that the Limey will finish the game," Stuart said.

And so it went.

Beharry berated Stuart, but cooled off when Stuart reminded him that he needed a ride home. Watkins held his breath, keenly aware that only he, Pops and Moses were left to bat.

Pierre pointed to Moses. "Somebody, pad him up."

Watkins gasped, and the sucking sound that Pops made indicated that he, too, couldn't believe that the kid was being sent in ahead of the veterans.

The sight of a fully padded up, helmeted Moses shuffling toward the wicket like an oversized R2-D2 from a Star Wars movie provided some comic relief all around.

"Our secret weapon," Pierre said to the Jamaica Rebels fielders.

"Remember your basics," the shrink, who had been coaching Moses on the side, told the boy, as Timmy walked backward in front of Moses, camera rolling.

The Jamaica Rebels crowded Moses, who, forgetting his basics, assumed a baseball stance and swatted the first ball away. It was a solid hit.

"Run Moses, run!" Sankar shouted, and Moses dropped his bat and ran. "The bat! The bat! Run with the bat!"

Moses turned to get the bat, tripped and fell. A fielder darted to the sticks, ball in hand, and knocked them over.

Moses came out grinning, although he hadn't scored.

"Next time, remember your bat is like an American Express card; never leave home without it," said the shrink.

"I'll remember," Moses said from somewhere behind the helmet.

"Where's Pops?" Pierre looked around. Minster stood directly behind him, already padded up. "Go on out."

Watkins told himself he was a team player. No big deal if he was sent in dead last.

Pops tilted on the way out, his limp more pronounced, his pace slower than normal. He and Napoleon consulted in the middle. Pops played forward, blocking in the meat of the blade a ball that appeared dead on. The ball went past a fielder. Pops and Napoleon ran for opposite ends of the carpet.

"Pops is off the mark," Pierre said, and recorded the run.

Watkins did the math in his head: Nine to tie, ten to win.

Stuart hand-delivered the ball to Zig-Zag, telling him that Napoleon had lasted too long, that it was time to "scatter his sticks."

Napoleon psyched himself up by taking off his gloves, cracking his knuckles, putting the gloves back on, bending his knees and swaying his body back and forth as though dancing to an exercise tape, then scanning the field and announcing to the bowler that he was ready.

"Come," he invited Zig-Zag. "Scatter my sticks."

Zig-Zag took a longer run, and flew in. The ball must have slipped from his hand because it went sky high. Napoleon waited, and waited, and waited with upraised bat for it to come down, and swung. The bat flew out of his hands. The ball dropped on top of the sticks, scattering all three. Even Napoleon joined in the universal laughter at the freak out.

Watkins looked toward Pierre. He was the last batsman, and should have headed out on his own, but Pierre had treated him with such disrespect he wasn't even sure that the captain wanted him to bat.

"Guess you might as well go in," Pierre said.

Watkins took offense to the way Pierre said it. The captain had in effect told him he had no illusions about his ability to score the needed ten runs, with or without Pops' help. Mentally, Pierre already had conceded the game. They might as well go home because the fat lady had sung.

His colleagues, however, didn't take it so lightly. They gave Watkins lots of unsolicited advice: Hold your bat this way, that way, and everywhichway. Advice on the type of bowling he could expect; advice that he should play defensive cricket; push forward as Pops had done the first ball he faced; don't play back; watch Zig-Zag because "he's tricky; a very crafty bowler"; and watch Long Man because "he pelts one every now and then" instead of turning his arm completely over.

"You can do it," Hankowsky said.

Watkins appreciated the encouragement.

Pops greeted him halfway and walked back with him to the wicket, wanting to know the strategy.

"We'll just play our natural game," Watkins said.

"Come on, old man," said Stuart. "Take your medicine and be done with it."

Like sharks at the smell of blood, the fielders who had walked off the field came back to help finish Fernwood off. They came to within seven feet, in front, sides and back of him, crouching, hands extended with palms open, expecting an easy, baby catch.

"Let's wrap it up," Stuart said to his men. "One ball for the old man. One and done."

Watkins felt strange. It had been such a long time since he had been out to bat. In his head, he still was at the top of his game. The moment of truth had arrived. He leaned forward, tapping the ground with his bat, psyching himself up.

Zig-Zag started his run, zigging and zagging, playing peek-a-boo behind Asquith before finally arriving at the bowler's mark. He showed Zig-Zag all three sticks, daring him to hit them, but he knew that the bowler would be aiming for a much, much larger target - his upper body. Watkins told himself he would block, push, and wait for the bad balls before going on the offensive. It was all in his hands. He could pull it out.

Everything he told himself was discarded when the ball arrived, dropping just short and rising nastily toward his belly button. Watkins stepped back, ignoring the advice to play forward, elevated himself on his toes to give himself room, and slapped at it. The ball crashed into the meat of the bat and sailed over the heads of second and third slips.

Watkins started to run, heard his colleagues screaming, "Don't run! Don't run! Don't spoil the shot by running!" and stopped. He looked back, and saw the fielders had given up the chase. As the ball rolled past the flag and Asquith signaled four runs, he raised his bat to his camp to acknowledge the applause.

"After all these years, you haven't forgotten!" the Black Chinaman roared.

"Frankie Worrell lives!" the shrink added, and Watkins thought it was quite a compliment to be compared to the fabled West Indian player.

Five to tie, six to win; I can do it, Watkins told himself.

The next ball was pitched up much closer to the bat. Watkins again moved back, giving himself room, but the ball didn't rise as high on the bounce, and, instead of moving away to his right, curled from the right into him. It was a beautiful delivery, dead on the sticks, and he was committed to playing the wrong stroke. He tried to recover by jabbing the bat down, fully expecting the ball to elude his willow and knock the sticks down. Instead he heard a cracking sound and saw the ball rocket through the gap between cover and short extra cover.

From the sidelines, it must have looked like a well-timed, meticulously executed power shot with the finesse of a pro, for his teammates were jumping up and down, screaming, "Shot, sah! Shot, sah!" and giving one another high-fives.

Fielding at silly-mid on, a few feet from the batsman, Stuart clapped and said, "Nice shot, old man."

Watkins nodded, perfunctorily, as though he did that sort of thing every time. "You ain't seen nuttin' yet," he murmured to himself.

He had racked up eight of the required ten runs with two swings of the bat and now he needed just one more to tie, and two to win. No problem.

Stuart asked the scorers the score. They confirmed it and Watkins saw he was about to get some respect: Stuart retreated a few paces and motioned his in-close fielders to spread out.

Clearly angered by the unexpectedly rough treatment by an unlikely batsman, Zig-Zag unleashed a beamer, the ball coming straight from the bowler's hand to his head. Watkins ducked safely. He sat, with a grin, on the carpet to catch himself. Pierre came onto the field to lodge a formal protest with Asquith, who promptly rebuked Zig-Zag.

Rising, Watkins saw two police car with lights rotating coming toward him from the parking lot. K-9 dogs sat on the back seats behind wire cages. Max Kruger trotted alongside like a Secret Service agent providing escort to a presidential motorcade. Scores of Little Leaguers and adults followed.

What conceivably could Kruger have told the cops to warrant the attack dogs?

The cars stopped on the edge of the carpet. Two uniformed officers alighted from one of the vehicles.

"Who's in charge here?" demanded one, a sergeant by his stripes, body bristling, eyes sweeping over the players.

Pierre ran up. "I'm the club's attorney."

The sergeant stuck his thumbs between his belt and clothes, and pushed out his chest. "Did I ask you your occupation?"

Pierre, wisely, didn't respond.

Other Fernwood players, spectators from both camps and the Little League battalion invaded the field.

"Well, Mr. Attorney, can I see your permit?" the sergeant said to Pierre.

Watkins caught Pierre's gaze and said, "We were assigned this field by Mr. Joe Sarubbi, the recreation director, pending reopening of the Fernwood Park."

The officer stared Watkins down. "Did I ask you a question?"

Watkins thought it obvious that, like Kruger, the officer hadn't come seeking explanations, but simply to kick them out. Unlike Kruger, he had the muscle to do it.

"If you don't have a permit, then this cricket game is over," the sergeant said.

Watkins weighed his options: Sarubbi had given the okay orally for Fernwood to use the field, but he had no proof of that. He doubted that Kruger had a permit, but that wasn't the issue right now. They could leave quietly and take the matter up with Sarubbi later, or refuse and risk being set upon by the K-9 dogs. But how real was that possibility? This, after all, was Fernwood, USA, at the start of the twenty-first century, not Mississippi or Alabama in the 1960s. Were the officers *that* crazy?

Kruger stepped to the sergeant's side. "I did warn you people," he said to Watkins.

A commotion erupted behind the Little Leaguers.

"TV Channel-8 coming through." Michael Hankowsky was pushing his way through the crowd. He had fashioned his shaggy hair into a ponytail, wore a blue and red blazer that was a couple sizes too large for him, and carried a wireless microphone. Timmy followed, camera on his shoulder.

The second officer made a rush toward Timmy. "No TV."

Timmy pointed the camera at him. The officer backed off, bringing up his hands to shield his face.

"We got a call about a race riot," Hankowsky said, pointing the microphone at the sergeant. "What can you tell us, officer?"

The sergeant glanced at the camera, then at Hankowsky. He did that several times. Hankowsky waited.

Watkins decided to play along. "There's no riot," he said. The microphone and camera were thrust into his face. "It seems that Mr. Sarubbi inadvertently scheduled the Fernwood Cricket Club and the Fernwood Little League to use the field at the same time. The officers are here to assist in resolving the matter. Peacefully."

"And who are you, sir?" Hankowsky said.

"Watkins," Watkins said. "Frederick Alfred Watkins, manager of the Fernwood Cricket Club."

Hankowsky was back in the officer's face with the mic as Timmy shifted the camera. "Is what Mr. Watkins said correct, sir? You are here to assist in the peaceful resolution of a scheduling conflict?"

The sergeant's Adam's apple went up and down. "That's right."

"No, it ain't right," Kruger said, and mic and camera shifted to him. "This field is the property of the Fernwood Little League. These people are trespassing. We don't have enough fields for our people, much less outsiders."

Watkins heard his teammates growl.

"Easy, everybody," Pierre said. "Let Watkins continue to deal with it."

"And what's your name, sir?" Hankowsky asked Kruger.

The snakelike lines were back on Kruger's dark-red face. "Do I know you?"

"You probably saw me on TV-8."

Kruger addressed the camera: "My name is Maximilian Kruger. I'm the president, manager and coach of the Fernwood Little League. And this," he added, turning to a young man with the crew cut hairstyle at his side, "is my son, Otto. He's my assistant."

"And do you, sir, Herr Kruger," Hankowsky said, "have proof that this field is the property of the Fernwood Little League or that these gentlemen from the Fernwood Cricket Club are outsiders?"

"We're Americans," Kruger snorted. "We don't need no proof. These people have been warned to leave the field or face arrest."

"Is that so, officer?" Hankowsky said. "Fernwood's finest are about to arrest a group of athletes on a Sunday afternoon, in the presence of their wives and children, for playing cricket in Fernwood? Is that the scoop for TV-8?"

The officer who had hidden his face from the camera said, "No one said anything about arresting anybody."

"This is America," Kruger said to him. "Baseball is the national sport. Nobody ever heard of croquet."

"Cricket," Pierre said.

"Whatever," Kruger said.

"We aren't here to arrest anybody," the sergeant said, in a suddenly take-charge voice. "We received a complaint. Like Mr. Watkins said, we are here to resolve what appears to be a scheduling conflict. Peacefully. We treat everybody fairly. That's the American way, and that's the way we do things in Fernwood."

"No, it ain't," Kruger said.

"And how do you intend to resolve it, officer?" Hankowsky asked.

Watkins said, "The matter easily can be resolved tomorrow."

"These athletes," Kruger replied, waving his arms at the jockeying youngsters, "have a league game to play. Not tomorrow, but now. If they don't, they lose points."

"We are finishing a league game," Watkins said. "We've been playing here since 1 o'clock. The game normally goes until 7 o'clock. Today we should wrap up by 4:30. Another couple minutes. Matter of fact, we need only one ball to wrap it up."

"What do you mean one ball?"

"One pitch."

"One pitch?" the sergeant said. "You mean one pitch and it's over?"

"That's right," Watkins said. "Should take no more than two minutes. The game would have been over had we not been interrupted."

The officer waved off the crowd. "Okay, everybody off the field so the players can complete their game."

Kruger grabbed the officer's arm. "What the hell are you doing? These people don't belong here."

"Pipe down, Max," the officer said. "They've got one pitch left." He turned to Watkins. "I'm taking you at your word. One pitch."

"One pitch should do it," Watkins said.

The officers began reversing their vehicles.

Kruger glared at Watkins. "You'll be hearing from the mayor on this."

"Goodbye, Max," Hankowsky said. "Don't forget to watch Channel 8 tonight."

"Zum Teufel mit dir!" Kruger said.

"And the same to you," the shrink said.

Watkins shook his head in disbelief at his friend and neighbor. "I don't believe you. Where did you get that blazer?"

"Borrowed it from your car." Hankowsky removed the rubber band and shook his hair loose. "Next time, make sure you get a permit. Once you get that permit, nobody can chase you off."

Pierre had another concern. "Why did you tell the officer we needed only one pitch?"

"Easy," Watkins said, relieved by the outcome. Hankowsky's quick thinking and daring had saved the day. Now, he could get on with the task of winning the game for Fernwood and going home to his waiting family. "We only need two runs, right? One to tie, and one to win. One swing of the bat should do it."

"But what if you swung and missed?"

"I won't," said Watkins. The assurance was more to himself than to Pierre.

The captain patted him on the back, something Watkins felt the skip should have done the first time around.

"Go ahead," Pierre said. "Bring the bacon home." He went up to Pops. "The moment the ball leaves the bowler's hand, start running. Get that? Run, no matter whether Watkins hits the ball or not."

"Don't have to tell me that, Skip," Pops said. "Common sense."

"You, also," Pierre said, returning to Watkins. "Run even if you miss the ball and the wicketkeeper collects it."

Stuart must have overheard Pierre's advice, because he brought the fielders in to cut off any attempt at a sharp run. He threw the ball to Zig-Zag and said, "Put everything into it." Then, on consultation with the bowler, Stuart asked four fielders to drop back just in case Watkins penetrated the ring of close-in fielders. They kept shuffling fielders around, like cards in a deck.

"Play ball!" the sergeant shouted from behind the flags.

Watkins tapped his bat and watched Zig-Zag come pounding in. Zig-Zag had carried the brunt of the bowling and should have been dead tired by now. But, like a veteran athlete toward the end of a grueling duel and with the outcome on the line, Zig-Zag was mustering up that reserve of energy for a strong finish. Watkins again steeled himself. The situation he faced wasn't unfamiliar to him. He had been there. Many times. One swing. One cracking sound when bat and ball collided head-on and the bacon was home. That's all it would take. One swing of the bat.

The air grew still, and Watkins saw that all off sides activities had been suspended. Everyone had taken up a vantage position behind the flags. Even the officers and the Little Leaguers seemed captivated. They stood with hands shading their eyes awaiting the outcome of this one pitch. Even the breeze had stopped blowing and the birds in the trees peered out. No commercial aircraft were beginning their descent into Philadelphia International Airport. Now, the sound of Zig-Zag's boots, intensifying like that of an oncoming buffalo stampede, dust flying behind them, the sound punctuated by the tap-tapping of the bat, like the percussionist in a big band, carrying the beat.

This is what it has come down to. Zig-Zag, him, and ten crouching fielders, and a little red ball that had lost its shine.

Then, Watkins had an unthinkable thought: What if he missed? From hero, he'd be the goat, hung in effigy, tarred and feathered for telling the officers that they needed only one pitch to finish the game. He could have asked for five to ten more minutes. That would have been plenty of time to score the two runs needed to win. In his arrogance he had asked for one pitch.

"Did you hear what he did?" they'd say, giggling like schoolgirls at that awkward age. "Told the officers all we needed was one pitch, then went and missed the damn ball." And, like good storytellers, they'd embellish the tale and by the time they were through, he'd be some buffoon.

The thought sent a chill through Watkins. He felt a panic attack coming on, and froze.

And now, Zig-Zag's arm came down and the ball was coming his way. It was a full toss, headed straight for the sticks. Watkins picked it up easily in flight, came out of his immobility and put his lumber to it. From where he stood, the ball appeared headed for the bushes for an automatic six runs. The bacon was home, three times over.

Pops, heeding Pierre's parting advice, ran toward him. "Come on!"

Fernwood's camp joined the entreaty: "Run! Run! Run!"

But Watkins stood there, like Reggie Jackson, mesmerized by the flight, feeling the power of the blast, and that certain warm glow, totally oblivious of Pops' entreaties and the screams from the Fernwood camp, "Run! Run! Run!"

Horror or horrors! What's going on here? There must have been a sudden air turbulence that pushed the ball back, for it wasn't going into the bushes anymore, but falling just short of the flags. It hit the ground.

Plop!

The ball must have landed in a very damp spot, for it didn't move after it fell. Simply sat there like a dud. He had just laid an egg. A big, fat, duck egg.

A Jamaica Rebels player dashed across the field and scooped the ball up. Here comes the long, hard throw toward the wicketkeeper's end. Watkins woke up then, and started running. But Pops, not wanting to be stranded and run out, had scrambled back to his end.

Watkins shouted, "Come on, man, let's go."

Pops again started toward him. As they were about to cross each other, Watkins looked back to see if the ball had arrived into the wicketkeeper's gloves. He must have turned his body the wrong way because Pops plowed into him and they went down.

They scrambled up and resumed running.

"The other way!" Fernwood's camp screamed. "The other way!"

Watkins didn't quite understand - until he saw the wicketkeeper hovering over the sticks waiting for the ball's arrival, and realized that he and Pops were headed back to their respective ends without crossing for a run.

The throw was dead on. It would have struck the sticks had the wicketkeeper not reached out to grab at it. The ball bounced off the gloves and continued past the wicketkeeper.

Watkins saw clearly the accidental contact of the wicketkeeper's pads and the sticks as the wicketkeeper grabbed for the ball, knocking one of the sticks down. That meant the ball was still alive and in play. The wicketkeeper, too, also recognized this because, instead of appealing for a run-out, he had tossed his right glove aside and began chasing the ball. The other Jamaica Rebels players apparently thought the ball had knocked the stick over, which meant that Watkins was out, for they were celebrating, lifting Zig-Zag and giving one another high-fives.

Watkins called Pops for a run. Pops, too, must have thought the game over, for he was walking off the field.

"Come on!" Watkins said. "Run!"

They crossed each other and completed the one run. Watkins calculated that the teams were now tied. One more needed to win. He started back, shouting to Pops to run the second one, even as Stuart and his teammates rejoiced. All except their wicketkeeper, who continued to chase the ball.

He and Pops crossed again, and Watkins thought there was time, for a third run. This would be an insurance run. Just in case the scorers, in their final tally, came up one short. It happens.

"Let's go, let's go," he urged on Pops, who stood leaning over his bat, blowing hard.

Pops saw him bearing down and shook his head, and spoke with his eyes: "Two's enough; I can't make another." But Watkins didn't stop, forcing his partner to run. Watkins made it safely down the wicket. Pops was still mid-carpet headed the other way. The wicketkeeper picked up and, without anyone backing up and not wanting to take a chance on throwing and missing the sticks, ran toward them, ball in hand.

Pops was closer and stood more than a fifty-fifty chance of getting there first. But the wicketkeeper, a man of great bulk but surprising agility, was bearing down faster. Watkins saw Pops' legs buckle, saw him stagger and go down, falling on both knees. But Pops had the presence of mind to thrust his bat forward.

The camera replays would show that Pops was propelled forward by his own momentum as he went down. In the final analysis, it didn't really matter how he got to the opposite end. The fact was the extended bat got there before the wicketkeeper knocked over the remaining two sticks with the ball.

Watkins ran to Pops, seated on the carpet, face dripping with sweat, breathing hard, but smiling.

"Did I make it?"

"You made it," Watkins said.

Pops flashed a broad, serene smile.

Watkins pulled him up, and embraced him. "We did it! We did it!"

The Jamaica Rebels had ended their celebration and were staring at them in puzzlement.

"We did it," Watkins said to Stuart. "We won."

Stuart laughed. "The game's been over a long time."

Only then did Watkins look at Asquith in Beharry's lab coat. The Englishman had his finger up, and Watkins got the uneasy feeling that it had been up a long time giving the game to Jamaica Rebels. He started to explain to Asquith what had happened, but the Englishman rooted up all three sticks at his end, signaling the end of the game, and began walking off.

Watkins walked ahead of the pack, trying hard to contain his anger. It was only a game, he reminded myself. These things do happen. His teammates awaited him with the same mystified look that Pops wore when he first pressed him to run. They all wanted to know what happened.

Watkins threw his bat down and tossed his gloves aside while explaining why he had forced Pops to keep running after everyone thought the game was over.

Napoleon said, "If you weren't out, why did the Limey put you out?"

"I guess he didn't see it." Watkins stood on the bleachers, unbuckling his pads. He also tossed those aside.

"Even so, he's supposed to be one of us," Napoleon said. "He's not supposed to put his own man out."

The general descended on the oncoming Asquith and related to him what Watkins said. Asquith wanted to hear from Watkins himself.

Watkins told him what happened. Asquith shrugged at the explanation. "I didn't see it."

"It doesn't matter whether you did or not," Napoleon said. "The fact is you aren't supposed to put your own men out."

"I don't cheat," Asquith said.

"You put on Beharry's umpire jacket and now you're sounding like him," said Napoleon.

"It ain't cricket to cheat," Asquith said, with proper indignation.

"You've been in the sun too long," Napoleon said.

"Fellers, cool it," Watkins said. He had cooled off, and realized it was wrong to have raised the issue. It only created dissention among their ranks, and it wasn't going to change the game's outcome.

Watkins watched the scorers erase the last three runs next to his name, and adjusted the final score. Instead of winning by two runs, they had lost by one.

Napoleon followed Asquith around, and the attacks on the Englishman grew more intense.

"So I made a blooper," Asquith said. "Now, bog off."

"Did they pay you off?" Napoleon said.

The Englishman faced the general. "You know, I don't have to put up with this."

Asquith grabbed his canvas bag off the aluminum stands and called out to his wife and daughters. Cindy, who had returned after giving Vijay Patel a ride home, had a little game going with her daughters and Moses.

"Get the girls," Asquith said to her. "We're leaving." He strode past the Fernwood players. "Bunch of ninnies!"

Cindy dropped the bat and trotted after her husband. "Shane!"

"Shane!" Napoleon echoed, in a singsong voice. "Come back, Shane!"

The Jamaica Rebels laughed. They had wandered over, inquiring about the food.

"The Limey sure has a hot head," Napoleon said.

Moses came up. He was back in his FUBU top. The boy wanted to know whether Watkins was a famous cricketer.

Watkins welcomed the distraction. "You've never heard of Frederick Alfred Watkins?"

The boy thought about it, and said, "Not really," but asked for his autograph anyway, and offered his mitt.

Watkins pulled out a bat from the kit and signed it instead: *To Moses, our Secret Weapon, All the best, Frederick A. Watkins.*

Moses beamed. "Thanks."

"That's a hundred-dollar bat," Napoleon said.

"It's an old bat we use during practice," Watkins said. "And you didn't pay dues to buy it."

A Little Leaguer came over and said his dad wanted them to remove the carpet in the middle of the field. White lines were being painted across the grass. Little Leaguers were warming up outside the lines. In the parking lot, Max Kruger, son Otto, and the police officers had their heads together between the two squad cars. The Krugers appeared to be giving the cops an earful.

Chong started to slink away but Pierre called his name, freezing him. He assigned the Black Chinaman to head up a four-member carpet-removal brigade.

"All latecomers must bring in the mat; that's the policy," Pierre reminded the lazy Barbadian. "Maybe next time you'll come out early enough to work on the wicket and put the mat out."

The pizza delivery boy arrived with the pies, sodas and supplies. Watkins placed the food and drink along the top rung of the aluminum stands.

"Visitors first," he said to Napoleon, but the Jamaican pace bowler continued to pile slices on his plate.

Watkins spotted Pops seated alone on the first rung of the stands, wiping his face with a handkerchief, still trying to catch his breath.

He took two slices over. "Here's to our hero."

Watkins felt a tap on his shoulder. It was Hankowsky, holding up a two-headed coin. He had found it in the grass. They confronted Beharry with the coin. The umpire was wolfing down another slice. He was minus his lab coat. His New York Knicks sweatshirt must have shrunk for it had retreated upward to expose a hole, presumably a button, in the middle of his hairy belly.

"That ain't mine," Beharry said. "You guys really trying to impugn my integrity."

"How can you impugn something you ain't got?" Napoleon said.

"But if you want to give it to me, I'll take it," Beharry said.

"I bet you would," Watkins said, and pocketed the coin.

Another tap on his shoulder.

"Timmy got it on tape," Hankowsky said.

"What does Timmy have on tape?"

"Pops sliding into first base," Hankowsky said. "I just looked at it on the monitor."

Watkins made the announcement. Hankowsky borrowed the scorers' table and placed it near the sliding door of his TV truck. He placed a TV monitor on the table. Players and spectators from both sides crowded around the monitor. Hankowsky ran the tape.

"Close," Beharry said. "But no cigar."

Pierre asked Hankowsky to run the tape again, in slow motion this time. He did, and froze the frame as the wicketkeeper's left pad came into contact with the sticks as he tried to grab the thrown-in ball, knocking over one of them. The ball was an inch or so from the wicketkeeper's gloves.

"You're right," Beharry said. "It was his pad that hit the sticks, not the ball. Pops wasn't out."

"Doesn't matter," Stuart said. "The game is over. Besides, you weren't the umpire then."

"I'm still the official umpire," Beharry told Stuart. "That means I adjudicate all disputes. If I say he's out, he's out; if I say he ain't, he ain't."

"Too much time elapsed," Stuart said.

"I decide that," Beharry said. "Fernwood wins."

Watkins felt an urge to kiss Beharry. In that one, bright, shining moment the umpire had wiped the slate clean of the gross injustices he had inflicted on Fernwood during the game. But he never got a chance. The Jamaica Rebels besieged and backed Beharry against the TV truck.

"What, you guys never heard of instant replay?" Beharry said.

"Instant replay, my ass!" Long Man shrieked, and pulled a bat from Fernwood's kit.

The Fernwood players intercepted Long Man. A brief, intense pushing and shoving followed. It ended suddenly when someone said, "Where did he go?"

Beharry had pulled a Houdini. People were raising their feet, as if expecting to find him flattened underfoot. The same voice that had raised the query about his whereabouts said, "There he is!"

Beharry had rolled under Pierre's pickup truck, had come up on the other side and was taking flight across the field in his mud-splattered outfit, weaving his way through a sea of Little Leaguers.

Long Man, bat in hand, took up the chase. The excitement proved too much for Singh's bulldog. The animal broke from its leash and chased after the two men. Long Man looked back, saw the dog coming and broke to the left, no doubt hoping to give the animal a clear path to Beharry. But the dog also broke left.

Singh ran after the dog, screaming in his native tongue.

Hankowsky offered Watkins a beer. The label said: *Jersey Devil*, and it had a picture of a red devil. "Time for a cold one, my friend. Special from my brother-in-law's micro-brewery in Philly."

Watkins drew Hankowsky's attention to the posted sign: "No drinking in the park, remember?" he said.

"Lighten up," Hankowsky said. "You're the man of the moment. You deserve a little libation."

"Not in the park."

"I've already passed out a few," Hankowsky said. "I'll make sure to collect the empty bottles."

A police officer approached. "Can I have a word with you?" he said to Hankowsky.

Caught with the bottle to his mouth, Hankowsky clumsily tried to conceal it behind his back. "What did I do?"

"Do you know Jennifer Barton?" the officer asked.

"The 11 o'clock anchor?" Hankowsky said. "Sure. I know Jenny."

"How well do you know her?"

"Real well," Hankowsky said. "We work on stories and hang out together at the Pen and Pencil Club in Philly."

"Is she as pretty in person as she appears on TV?"

For a moment, Hankowsky appeared stumped.

"Hope you don't mind my asking," the officer said.

"Prettier," Hankowsky said. "You see only her talking head. You should see the rest of her." He drew a Coca-Cola bottle with his hands.

"Goddamn!" The officer handed Hankowsky a card. "Patrolman Brian Galloway, Fernwood's finest. Mind giving her my card?"

Hankowsky glanced at it. "Sure thing."

"Tell her I have a hot tip for her," said Galloway.

"I'll see that she gets it."

"Much appreciated."

Watkins watched the exchange in disbelief.

Hankowsky cupped his mouth to stifle his laughter at the departing Galloway. "He wants to give our Jenny a hot tip. He and another four million male viewers."

"For a moment, I thought...." Watkins began.

Watkins heard a scream and saw a commotion on the other side of the bleachers. Running up, he observed Pops lying on his side, an empty flask in one hand, and the paper plate minus the pizza slices in the other.

Pierre rolled Pops over on his back. Pops' eyes were half-opened but vacant. Watkins knelt, felt his wrist and got a pulse. "We've got to get him to the hospital. Somebody, get the cops."

"He was sitting on the edge of the bleachers, and just rolled over," said the young woman who had screamed. She was about nineteen, with long, braided hair, and Jamaican by her accent.

Patrolman Galloway pushed through the crowd. He felt Pops' wrist, and radioed for an ambulance. The patrolman then tried to take the flask away but Pops wouldn't let go. The officer pulled out a notebook and Watkins found himself being peppered with questions about Pops' identity and medical history. He was still answering questions when the ambulance arrived.

Watkins looked on with increasing guilt as the medics took Pops' blood pressure, placed an oxygen mask over his face, and eased him onto a stretcher and into their vehicle.

Pierre and the shrink followed the ambulance in the captain's pickup.

The Jamaica Rebels players began leaving, expressing hope that "the old man" would be okay, then berating the missing-in-action Beharry for reversing the outcome in what they regarded as an act of revenge on his part for taking him out of the game.

"How could he let a rat's ass team like you guys beat us?" Stuart wondered aloud.

"Hey, crybabies," Napoleon said to him. "Have a nice trip home."

Stuart replied with a gesture with his middle index finger.

"No, no, baby, you don't do that to me." Napoleon sprinted toward him.

Stuart dropped his bag and put up his fists.

Watkins stepped in Napoleon's path, and planted a hand on his chest. "Don't! We've already won the game. Show some class."

Napoleon shoved him aside with one hand, and stuck his face into Stuart's. "Do that again!" he challenged the Jamaica Rebels captain.

Stuart threw a punch that Napoleon either didn't see coming or was too slow to stop. It landed on his left jaw. Napoleon staggered sideways.

Watkins held him up. "Come on, guys. None of this is called for."

Napoleon wiggled free and was back in Stuart's face, wagging a finger and speaking in a voice so emotionally charged and with an accent that had become so thick that Watkins didn't get it. But he distinctly heard the words "gun" and "shoot." Napoleon then wiped out the Jamaica Rebels with an imaginary machine gun before retreating.

Watkins was at a loss. "What did he say?"

"He said he's going to get his shotgun and come back and shoot everybody," Zig-Zag translated.

Watkins weighed the threat. Unsporting behavior wasn't unusual during hard-fought games. Why, even he, in his superstar days, had been known to kick down the wicket and verbally abuse the umpire after particularly egregious calls against him. But these types of schoolboy theatrics tended to be heat-of-the-moment reactions. Once the game was over, and the food arrived, the mood would go from threatening to jovial. And when time came to part, there would be handshakes all around, with the traditional comment of "Nice game."

In his long experience with the game, Watkins could recall no situation where disputes degenerated to threats of mass murder.

Was Napoleon grandstanding? The Jamaica Rebels evidently thought not, for there was a sudden, mass exodus of players and supporters. As word of Napoleon's threat spread, Fernwood's camp also emptied out in a hurry.

Watkins looked up after making sure all the team's gear was secured and found himself alone at the bleachers. He headed for his wagon, straining under the weight of the bag.

Surajit, fully recovered, was in the driver's seat of the wagon, listening to the radio. Hankowsky had dumped the blazer on the back seat. Watkins put the bag in the wagon. He put his street clothes back on and dialed home.

No answer.

He reckoned that after having dinner without him, Maggie and Stephen had taken Edward over to Mrs. Alvarez, and Gina had accompanied them. It would be at least three more hours before they headed back to Manhattan. Perhaps he could make it up by taking them out for ice cream, instead of taking home dessert. But first, he needed to find out about Pops' condition.

A mile or so down the boulevard, Watkins drove past a little man in a New York Knicks sweatshirt, white lab coat slung over his left arm, walking eastbound along the shoulder of the road. He stopped, rolled his window down, and waited for the pedestrian to come up.

"Jump in the back," he told umpire Beharry. "I'll give you a ride to the bus stop."

******

A fter dropping an ever-so-grateful Beharry off at the bus terminal, Watkins drove to Southern New Jersey Hospital, Fernwood Division.

The receptionist at the information booth tapped into her computer and reported finding nothing on a newly admitted patient named Harold Richardson Minster. Watkins suggested she call up to Intensive Care, and sure enough, Pops had been taken straight to the unit. The attending physician, a Dr. Deshpande, gave the okay for him to come up with Surajit.

Watkins fingered his visitor's badge on the ride up. Pops' admittance to a floor normally off-limits to visitors made him doubly on edge. He found Dr. Deshpande in a small office-reception area near the elevator speaking to Pierre and Sankar. He was a small Indian man, about fifty, in green scrubs, a stethoscope around his neck and a file folder in his hands.

Pierre introduced the doctor and asked, "Do you remember him?"

The face was vaguely familiar.

"You look the same," Deshpande said, with an easy yet reserved smile.

The voice brought it back. A former club member. One of many foreign students who came and went during the early days when the cricket club was more of a social organization, providing comfort and reassurance for their diverse group in a new culture with which they all had difficulty coming to grips.

"Shekhar," Watkins said. "Shekhar Deshpande. Opening bat. Scored a century in your first game. Got us all excited, then vanished."

The smile broadened and the leathery face was boyish again.

"He also remembers Pops," Pierre said.

"I do," Deshpande said. "His spicy Jamaican beef patties were a treat."

"How is he?" Watkins asked.

The smile receded and the physician's voice grew subdued as he related what he had just told Pierre and Sankar: Pops had suffered a massive heart attack and was in a coma.

"He wore a pacemaker; did you know that?" Deshpande asked.

Watkins didn't. Neither did he know that Pops was diabetic; or about the steel pin that kept together a hip that broke when he fell on his icy concrete driveway after a night out drinking a few winters back; or his kidney problem; high blood pressure; or emphysema, though he should have suspected it from the chain-smoking and persistent coughing and wheezing.

Watkins braced for the worst. "What's the prognosis, doctor?"

"Miracles do happen." Deshpande's gaze shifted to the folder, giving Watkins time to compose himself. "According to his files, he has a wife, Wilhelmina Minster. Has anyone contacted her, or is that something the hospital should be doing?"

Watkins accepted responsibility for contacting Wilhelmina Minster.

Pierre handed Deshpande his business card. "Give me a call if you ever get the yen to play cricket again."

Deshpande smiled, noncommittal.

"Do you ever miss the game?" Watkins asked.

"Not really," the doctor said.

Watkins couldn't fathom how someone that talented with the bat could walk away from the game and not look back.

Riding the elevator down with his teammates, Watkins expressed the guilt he felt about having dragged Pops out. Pierre sought to deflect the blame, noting that he was the one who included Pops in the lineup.

"But you know what," the captain continued, "if he had his choice of dying, I think that's the way he'd want to go."

That thought didn't ease the pain any.

Darkness had fallen when he pulled into Pops' driveway in the Village.

Watkins rang the doorbell at the Minsters' rancher and inhaled deeply. How did the military people do it? First express sympathy, then give the bad news, or vice versa? Or did their appearance at some ungodly hour speak for itself?

Inside, a dog barked.

"Shut up!" a woman said, and Watkins wasn't sure whether she was yelling at the dog or him.

A light above the door went on, and the door was pushed open halfway. Wilhelmina Minster, hair plaited in rows and in a loose-fitting flowered dress, drew back at the sight of him, a serpent poised to strike, her chin becoming three uneven rows of flesh.

Watkins forgot his words.

Mrs. Minster thrust her head forward. Watkins retreated to the first of the three steps, pulling Surajit with him. Mrs. Minster looked past them, to their left, right, over their heads to the street, then back at him.

"Where's Harold?" she demanded.

Watkins couldn't get the words out.

"Spit it out!" she said.

He tried, and choked.

"Send you to beg for him, did he?" she said. "Wait till I get my hands on him."

"Harold suffered a heart attack after the game." He didn't know whether he shouted it out, but it sounded that way to his ear. "He's in intensive care at the hospital. I can drive you there and bring you back, if you wish."

Her eyes widened. She hissed. At the very least, he expected her to curse him, simply explode, spew out all the venom she had built up for him over the years, her church upbringing notwithstanding. He was prepared to take it. She would have been justified in accusing him of sending her husband to his deathbed, headed straight for Hades. He would have had no defense. But she didn't say a word. Simply stared and hissed, and seemed to grow larger as she sucked in more air than she let out, and just when she appeared about to pop, silently retreated.

The door remained open. Had she forgotten to close it? Or did it mean she would be right back? She returned instantly in a dark coat over the dress, and holding a scarf.

Watkins opened the front door of his wagon on the passenger side. She stepped around him and let herself into the back, behind the driver's seat. Her action may have spooked him, or maybe he had seen too many gangster movies, for he wondered why she carried the scarf in her hand and chose to sit directly behind him.

"You might want to sit on the other side," he said. "You'd get a more comfortable ride."

Those piercing eyes.

"Then again, it's only a short drive," he said.

Nonetheless, Watkins adjusted the rearview mirror, and drove with one eye on the road, the other on the reflection in the mirror, one hand on the wheel, the other protecting his throat. Mrs. Minster was silent throughout the drive.

He dropped her off at the main entrance of the hospital. Several of his teammates emerged with long faces. They attempted to speak to Mrs. Minster, but she brushed past. He waited in the No Parking zone near the entrance.

"That's one scary lady," Surajit said.

"She's just angry," Watkins said. "With good reason. Do you think we should go in?"

"Nope."

It would have been the right thing to do. At least make the effort to communicate rather than wait here in the semi-darkness like a dispassionate taxi driver, but instincts told him the boy was right. They should keep their distance. For now.

Watkins called home.

Busy.

The visit lasted twenty minutes.

Mrs. Minster remained silent on the way back. She got out the moment he pulled up in the driveway and came to his window. "I hope you are satisfied now!"

Watkins watched her enter the house and pull the front door shut. The front light went out.

Satisfied!

Cricket was Pops' life, the one thing that brought him sheer joy. He remembered the way Pops shook with excitement that morning when told to get his whites. He relived the moment of that last, insurance run, with Pops seated on the carpet, smiling serenely. Yes, he was satisfied that he had played a role in making the old man come alive.

But now Pops was in a coma and his wife was holding his teammates, him in particular, accountable. Was it worth it?

"If he had his choice of dying, that's the way he'd want to go," Pierre had said.

Was that too selfish a way to look at it? What about Mrs. Minster? Didn't she count? Was she just to be brushed off as a nag who stood between Pops and the boys? Couldn't there have been a compromise somewhere?

And how was that situation any different from his? He loved the game, and he also loved his wife. Why couldn't he have both?

It was almost 10 o'clock when he turned into Gardenia Court after dropping off the boy at the Sunrise Motel. His front porch light was on and neighbors were milling about his driveway and lawn.

"Is that his wagon?" he heard Mrs. Alvarez ask.

"That looks like it," said Mrs. Hutton.

"It's him!" confirmed Mrs. Bates.

Watkins pulled up behind Gina's BMW. Gina appeared in the doorway. A tiny squeal of delight escaped her lips. She began running toward him. About ten feet away, she stopped as if hitting an invisible wall. She turned and ran back into the house.

Watkins stood, confused.

"Do you know how much trouble you've caused your wife?" Mrs. Alvarez said.

"You ought to be ashamed of yourself!" snarled Mrs. Meredith.

"Men!" huffed Mrs. Sandiford. "They're all the same!"

"Go to her," said Mrs. Hutton.

The house lights went out.

Watkins went from room to room, turning on lights. He eventually found Gina seated on the armchair in a corner of the living room, half hidden by the giant artificial fig tree. Her hands were in her lap and she was wringing them, her eyes downcast.

"What's the matter?" Watkins dropped to his knees and took her hands in his, the way he had done when he proposed marriage. She continued doing her Lady Macbeth routine. "Is it Maggie? The baby?" He thought the worst. Tragedy finally had struck, a tragedy that wouldn't have happened had he been a more responsible husband, father and grandfather. "What is it?"

Gina's gaze met his. Her eyes glistened with tears. She suddenly reached out, pulling him to her, burying her head in his chest and throwing her arms around him.

He held her close. She was shaking. "Tell me!"

"I thought you were dead," she said.

"Dead!" He held her shoulders and pushed her back. "What made you think I was dead?"

"There was this story on TV, a cricket game, Fernwood and the Jamaica Rebels...."

Between the sobs, Gina told about a call she had received from Mrs. Hutton about a TV-8 Eyewitness News broadcast not long after Maggie and Stephen had left with the baby. The story was about spring fever manifesting itself with an explosion of activities across the Delaware Valley. The announcer said tragedy struck during a cricket game in Fernwood. There was a film of two men running, colliding, and then running again, then one of the men falling. The men got up and resumed running, and one of them appeared to stumble and fall. His name was mentioned: Frederick Alfred Watkins. The report didn't make clear who was who, and Mrs. Hutton couldn't tell because both men wore helmets. The fallen cricketer was lifted into an ambulance on a stretcher and Mrs. Hutton still couldn't tell whether it was him because the player was wearing an oxygen mask. The Hankowskys weren't in. She had tried to reach the TV station but couldn't get through. She and the neighbors had been calling area hospitals. None reported having a patient named Watkins. She called several of the club regulars but they hadn't been to the game. By 9 o'clock she had become convinced it was he, because he never got home this late after a home game.

"I tried reaching you several times," he said. "Either no one answered or the line was busy."

"Why didn't you leave a message?"

"I should have."

"So, where were you?"

"At the hospital." He rose. "The other player, the one who fell, was Pops. He suffered a heart attack. He's in a coma."

Watkins didn't wait for her response. He headed straight for the hot tub. He sank into the churning water and closed his eyes. At some point he became aware of her standing over him.

"I'm sorry I ruined your day," he said. "I'll call Maggie and Stephen and apologize. I'll make it up to them."

"I thought you'd organize the game and be back home early for your grandson, if not anyone else," she said.

"Please, don't harass me. I really don't feel too good right now."

For a long time, she was silent.

"The church is holding a breakfast meeting tomorrow to discuss plans for our annual picnic," Gina announced. "You're coming out with me. I'll ask Arty to begin the meeting with a special prayer for Mr. Minster's recovery."

"That would be nice." He appreciated her concern. Gina had known Pops for as long as he did.

"And you'll join the men's choir, as you said you would," she said.

That was an edict, but one with which he could live.

"Things are going to be different," Gina said. "Now that you've taken care of the communications problem and gotten your cricket team started on its new season, you're going to start acting your age, and acting responsibly toward your family."

The telephone rang.

It was the first of several calls they would receive throughout the night from members of the cricketing community from New York to California, all wanting an update on his condition after viewing Hankowsky's convoluted reporting of the tail end of the game, a report that somehow ended up on ESPN sports network.

Gina fixed him dinner, baked chicken and vegetables, but all he wanted after the hot soaking was to lie down.

"I don't know what got into you." She sat on the edge of the bed, applying baby oil to his back, and massaging. "You'll be fifty-five in a week, a senior citizen practically..."

He drifted off to the sound of her chiding voice and soothing hands. It had been quite a day.

EWART ROUSE

STICKY WICKET
Vol. 2

watkins
fights back

NOW AVAILABLE

Printed in the United States
202639BV00003B/1-24/P

9 789768 202406